WARBUCK

Army scout Buff McCall, son of a Scottish buffalo hunter and a Cheyenne squaw, is a man of mixed loyalities. His ten-year service with the army has made him privy to army ways. But when the government reneges on their agreement with the Indians, Buff deserts and joins the Sioux to defend the Black Hills. Now he is Warbuck, a Sioux warrior. Matters soon become complicated with the arrival of Charlie Norris, whose father had been killed during a raid. A problem indeed!

Books by Curt Longbow
in the Linford Western Library:

THE LAND GRABBERS
THE MAN FROM SOCORRO

CURT LONGBOW

◆

WARBUCK

Complete and Unabridged

LINFORD
Leicester

First published in Great Britain in 1999 by
Robert Hale Limited
London

First Linford Edition
published 2000
by arrangement with
Robert Hale Limited
London

British Library CIP Data

Longbow, Curt
  Warbuck.—Large print ed.—
Linford western library
1. Dakota Indians—Fiction 2. Western stories
3. Large type books
I. Title
823.9′14 [F]

ISBN 0–7089–5691–2

Published by
F. A. Thorpe (Publishing)
Anstey, Leicestershire

Set by Words & Graphics Ltd.
Anstey, Leicestershire
Printed and bound in Great Britain by
T. J. International Ltd., Padstow, Cornwall

This book is printed on acid-free paper

'Friend and brother, it was the will of the Great Spirit that we should meet together this day. He orders all things, and he has given us a fine day for our council. He has taken his garment from before the sun, and caused it to shine with brightness upon us; our eyes are opened, and we see clearly; our ears are unstopped, and we have been able to hear distinctly the words you have spoken; for all these favours we thank the Great Spirit and Him only . . . '

Excerpt from a speech made by Chief Red Jacket of the Iroquois at a meeting in Buffalo, New York, in 1805.

1

The detachment of soldiers was three days out of Fort Laramie and it would be several days before they came to Piney Ridge, where they were to set up camp and prepare to cut a road through the wilderness all the way to the Black Hills, constructing forts along the way for the troops following behind.

Buff McCall was uneasy. He and his fellow scout rode ahead of the detail, watching out for any suspicious moves from the Sioux. All was quiet and he didn't like it.

He glanced back at the column, headed by Colonel Harry Carrington, a seasoned officer who'd survived many Indian attacks. He looked confident and the men behind him rode easily.

It was a long column, for they were bringing with them all the equipment needed to build a temporary camp, wagons loaded with stores, tools, tents, a Gatling gun on a specially reinforced wagon for defence of likely sorties and the usual military chuck wagon, the only luxury in a soldier's life.

His eyes raked the surrounding hills, the uneasy feeling of being watched, sending prickles up and down his spine. He knew there were eyes watching their progress across the plain. He didn't like it.

He turned to the Sioux scout beside him.

'Do you feel anything, Fish Eye?'

Fish Eye turned slowly in his saddle and looked about him and then back grimly at Buff McCall.

'You feel it too? This very bad medicine. No like.'

'You think we should take a look?'

Fish Eye nodded. 'Bad place coming up. I know how Chief Red Cloud thinks. He good man and not want fight, but he must protect Black Hills for all red men.'

2

'Right. I'll go back and consult big chief. You keep your eyes well skinned, old son.' He grinned at the taciturn scout as he wheeled his mount and trotted back to the colonel.

'Sir,' he gave the colonel a sloppy salute. It was a gesture to the man and not to his military position. As a scout he was not under military discipline. 'I don't like the quiet. Would suggest Fish Eye and myself to fan out and do some scouting, just to be on the safe side?'

'Well now, McCall, that's what you are, a scout. So get out there and ease that tickle along your backbone, if it makes you happy.'

He put up a hand, and the detail stopped behind him. He looked up at the sun high in the sky.

'We may as well take a break until you both return. He waved a hand and his captain moved forward to join them. 'Captain, we're making a halt. The scouts are going foraging. I take it Fish Eye shares your misgivings, McCall?'

3

'Yes, sir. We expected Chief Red Cloud to put up some resistance. After all, he was angry when he heard the news of the new forts to be built right across to the Black Hills.'

'Hmm,' rasped the colonel. 'Maybe we should ride on full alert at all times.'

'Would be wise, sir. The Sioux are crafty swine, sir.'

'You should know, McCall!'

McCall flushed. 'My mother was Cheyenne, sir, not Sioux. There's a hell of a difference!'

Colonel Carrington snorted. 'They're all red bastards, McCall, but you couldn't help who your mother was! Right, then get to it, mister, and be careful. We don't want to start an incident!'

McCall choked his anger at the colonel's slur. Someday he would make him eat his words. He schooled his features and gave a flippant salute.

'Sir!' He wheeled his horse, galloped

onwards and only drew rein when he joined Fish Eye.

'Well?'

'I'll kill that bastard, someday!'

Fish Eye looked at him with some amusement and shook his head. 'Not before you find and kill the white man responsible for your mother's death or the Sioux brave who killed your father. I know you, Buff McCall. The only reason you are scout is to find them. The colonel can wait. Now we ride, yes?'

They lengthened their stride and rode together. When the terrain became dappled with rocks and boulders they split, McCall turning off to the left and Fish Eye to the right. Soon they were alone and now McCall moved cautiously as he entered a gulley, thinking this would be a good place to ambush a wagon train.

He dismounted, tying his horse to a stump of a tree, and moved cautiously ahead, climbing as he went.

He sweated, removing the army issue

wide-brimmed black hat and wiped his brow. He wore his coarse black hair long, tied back with a piece of red rag. He was Indian dark, more like his mother than his father, but he had his father's tall muscular frame. He wore Indian moccasins over deerskin pants for comfort and his well-worn jerkin was fringed and decorated with porcupine quills, a gift from a Cheyenne woman, many moons ago. Under it, he wore an army issue shirt of thick flannelette. His hat and his shirt were the only indications of his service to the military, except for the handgun hanging from a holster on his broad belt, and the Spencer rifle he carried at all times.

He still relied on the broad Bowie knife he carried in a sheath at his left side. That was his friend and saviour. He felt stark naked when he didn't have it on his person.

Now he scrambled upwards and peeped over a ledge to the valley below.

That was when he saw the Indian sitting on horseback, as still as a graven image, the sunlight glinting on his lance's tip winking and glowing as the brave stared down into the valley from the other side. McCall looked down and espied the small caravan. He counted six wagons and a small remuda of horses following behind. He saw the wheel tracks meandering across the grass.

The fools! Didn't those overlanders know there was much unrest at this time? He reckoned their destination was the Black Hills, for since Custer had discovered gold dust in his horse's hooves, there had been a steady trickle of prospectors and get-rich-quick merchants trying their luck in those sacred hills of the Indian tribes.

Even as he watched the Indian's arm came up in a sweeping wave and there appeared on the skyline a row of Indians. They were dressed for war.

He watched as they came thundering

down the steep slopes to the valley floor below, yelling their battle cries, and rode around the pitiful caravan in ever decreasing circles.

The puffs of blue-grey smoke wafted up into the sky. As McCall crawled away the acrid smell of cordite was in his nostrils.

The Sioux were on the prod. Chief Red Cloud was making his protests. They would be lucky to get to Piney Ridge and luckier still if they ever made camp.

Buff McCall shook his head. There were going to be many dead men before they got the forts built right across the country to the Black Hills. He wished the men behind those desks in Washington would come themselves and see the mess they were making for the army by coming up with hare-brained schemes. They should listen to the Indians. There were better ways than war to enforce what they wanted.

Chief Red Cloud was bound to go to war, bringing in the Cheyenne and the other tribes who held the Black Hills sacred.

McCall shivered. He had a presentiment. He must choose whether he was a white man or a Cheyenne brave.

He scrambled down the rocks and mounted his horse. He must get back to the colonel and report the situation. Let him decide whether they were to make a detour and help the stupid white folk, or carry on to Piney Ridge. It would be his decision.

2

There was no sign of Fish Eye as he rode back at breakneck speed to the detachment who were lounging around small campfires, their horses hobbled and feeding from nose-bags.

Colonel Carrington stood up from his folding chair and came before his camp table, which he used as an office and plotting-board when on manoeuvres.

'Well? Any sign of action?'

McCall dismounted and a trooper led his horse away to rub down before feeding and watering. McCall knew that the blacksmith riding with them would look him over for wear and tear on his shoes.

'Sir, there's a small wagon train on its way to the Black Hills. At this moment it is staving off a band of hostiles.'

'Hell and blast! I thought all travel

was suspended in this part of the country until we got the forts organized!' I suppose I'll have to send a detail.' He shouted for Captain Platte, who came running.

'Sir!'

'McCall reports Indians attacking a wagon train. Where abouts are they, McCall?'

'On the other side of that ridge, Colonel. It's a three hour ride but there's plenty of trail to get into that valley, sir. It's a matter of taking a short cut.'

'How many Indians?'

'A dozen or twenty, I should say.'

'And how many in the wagon train?'

'Can't be certain, sir, I counted six wagons, and there was a small herd of horses with them. Maybe the Indians were after them.'

'You think Red Cloud is on the prod?'

McCall shrugged. 'More like some of his braves trying to prove themselves. The whole nation is up in arms. It wouldn't take much for the situation to get out of hand.'

'Captain, we can't ignore the news. I want you and Sergeant Button to take a detail of twenty men and sort out these red bastards and arrange for the wagon train to join us, if there's any survivors, that is. Maybe we'll be too late.'

'Not by the way the defenders were firing, sir.'

'Good. Then get to it, both of you. How long will it take for you to get the men ready, Captain?'

'Half an hour, sir and we'll be on our way.'

'Right! Then send down the line for Lieutenant Saunders and tell him to get his ass up here. Corporal Fairbrother will have to keep the stragglers up to scratch.'

Captain Platte chose the most seasoned Indian fighters in the troop, and the men, bored with the monotonous journey, welcomed the break. They were men more used to action than discipline.

McCall welcomed the change. He got on well with James Platte who never cast snide remarks about his parentage. Platte lent him one of his own horses, which was fresh and raring to go.

They travelled fast, and the standard-bearer's pennant fluttered in the breeze. It was easy cutting a way through the high boulders, the ground smooth and sandy where, long years ago, water had cut a passage.

They came out into the valley on a high prominence and looked down towards the valley floor. The six wagons were now drawn in a tight circle. Inside were the horses, milling around, their excited neighing mingling with the sounds of yells from the Indians and spasmodic gunfire.

McCall saw at a glance that the first attack had been repelled. There were two horses in the tight circle prone on the ground. They had been dragged to plug up spaces between the wagons. There were several bodies lying around the wagons, proving that those inside knew how to use their weapons. One feathered corpse lay supine over a wagon shaft. By God, it had been a near thing, McCall thought, if an invader could manage to get so close!

He nodded to Captain Platte who gave the order to his bugler, in a cold, clipped voice, to sound the charge.

It was then that they saw the Indians, who'd been behind a ridge, gallop forth and begin their next onslaught.

'By God, they figure to do as much damage as they can before we get down to them!' the captain yelled. 'Let's have at 'em, lads!' The bugler sounded the charge and McCall felt the thrill of it as the horses' hooves thundered down the valley.

Then troopers met Indians and the bullets flew. There came a renewed volley from the besieged men and a whole lot of cheering.

McCall emptied his handgun, then, thrusting it back into its holster, brought out his Bowie knife. He struck

14

out as red bodies came at him. He felt a knife scraping his upper arm and the stickiness of blood but it meant nothing. He cut and stabbed until at last there was only one brave between him and the circle of wagons.

He felt the red man seize his arm and pull him from his horse. He tried in vain to shake him off but the Indian was supple and skilled in hand-to-hand fighting. They fell together, McCall underneath with the Indian straddling him. He saw the arm upstretched, the bloodied knife glinting in the sun. It was a good day to die, he thought, and then glanced at the face above his own. It was a hard, carved out of teak kind of face with fanatical eyes and the war paint of the Cheyenne on his cheek bones.

But what made his blood run cold and sent the adrenalin flowing in his veins was the certain knowledge that he'd seen this man before.

It was like seeing history all over again, but this time it wasn't his father being straddled by his killer but himself! His hand closed on the fist holding the knife and with a gigantic kick funnelled by a rush of hatred, he heaved the Indian over his head and let the man's weight send him crashing down. Then, twisting like an eel, McCall was up and throwing himself on the winded man.

'You're Cheyenne! One of Little Fox's Quick Stingers!'

The Indian's mad eyes gazed proudly up at McCall.

'Yes, what of it?'

'You killed the buffalo hunter called Old Buff McCall?'

'Yes. But that was many moons ago. Why do you ask?'

'He was my father.'

The Indian shrugged. 'So? It was your bad luck!'

'Why did you kill him?'

'Because he wasn't welcome in our village. Because the soldiers came and massacred our women and children and old ones while we braves were out hunting. He had to die!'

16

'He was not a soldier!'

'He was a buffalo hunter which was just as bad. He and others like him killed for killing's sake. He was a bad man.'

'He was my father, and for that you die!'

Then came the first hint of fear in the Indian's eyes as the broad sharp-bladed knife came down and slit his throat. He choked and gurgled, drowning in his own blood.

McCall rolled away as the blood spurted. He was drenched in it. Dazed, he cleaned the knife on the Indian's breechclout and stood up. All had gone quiet and he realized that those Indians who were still alive had retreated. Captain Platte was talking to a bunch of men from the wagon train.

He passed a shaking hand over his eyes. All his life he'd waited to meet up with the Indian who'd killed his father. The painted face had haunted his dreams since childhood. He couldn't believe it! The Great Spirit had at last answered his prayers.

He looked down at the bloodied face, already covered in flies attracted by the sweet stench of blood. The buzz sickened him and he moved away. If only he'd been able to find the man who'd killed his mother, then maybe his life would have turned out differently.

The captain turned to him as he drew near. 'I think Red Cloud's braves have had enough. We can rejoin the detachment.'

'They weren't Sioux. They were a band of Cheyenne Quick Stingers, coming into the territory to cause mayhem, and perhaps to persuade the army to believe it's all Sioux doing. After all, the Black Hills are just as sacred to the Cheyenne and other tribes as to the Sioux.'

'You think that, McCall?'

'I know that. Even when the tribes are at war with each other the Sioux allow access to the sacred places. After all, the Great Spirit does not exclude any tribe who wishes to worship.'

Captain Platte frowned. 'You believe all that rubbish about a Great Spirit?'

'Why not, sir? You believe in a Christian God. We all believe something and, most important, the Indian tribes believe in the sanctity of the Black Hills.'

'You think there will be a general uprising?'

'Undoubtedly, sir. This breaking of the government treaty signed at Fort Laramie is not going to make the five great nations respect the government or the white man.'

'What do you think will happen, McCall?'

McCall shrugged. 'If I was Chief Red Cloud, I'd send runners and form a great Council and make talk, but pride would make them go to war!'

'And you think Fish Eye thinks the same?'

'Of that I am sure. Already he talks of going back to his village and offering his services.'

'Does he, by God! He's too valuable to lose! I think we should make haste and catch up with Colonel Carrington. As for these miners, they have a choice. They can come with us and help build the military camp at Piney Ridge, or go back to where they came from. They're a responsibility and a damned nuisance!'

There were casualties among the miners: three dead and one not expected to live through the night. McCall saw with relief that there were no women amongst them. Eleven men, and one of them just a boy, and not one of them used to carrying a gun, never mind using one.

He looked at the exhausted group. Some were bloodied and some were white-faced and drawn, half-starved by the look of them.

Their wagons were filled with food staples and mining implements. The whisper of gold to be picked up, and of the rivers of the Black Hills all awash with gold dust had caused a gold fever amongst men who'd spent their lives digging coal or lead and only earning enough to survive and have a Saturday night blow-out in some sleazy saloon. These men had had the courage to go after their Eldorado, and make their dreams come true. McCall respected them, even though he knew they were foolish.

He approached the bunch of men standing together, debating the problem of the captain's pronouncement. They could go back, or they could join the labouring party. Two of the older men were for going back. The rest were adamant that they should go on. The lone boy amongst them was silent.

, 'After all, we'll make Piney Ridge with the soldiers. We can help build the camp and then later, maybe we can go on.'

'You're a hell of a way from the Black Hills.' They all turned to look at McCall. 'You've got to travel through Wyoming. At least you'd hit the Bozeman Trail, but it's dangerous.

Indians all the way.'

'You been in those hills, mister? Is it true about gold nuggets lying on the ground?'

McCall laughed and shook his head. 'I was there as a child. I saw no gold. There was a drought. My mother was Cheyenne.' He stopped and glared about him, waiting for a snide look. None came. 'The whole village went to the Black Hills and we sought out the place of the Rainmaker. It was a holy place and there were prayers and singing and then came the Raindance and there was a fire in the middle of the great basin, which was surrounded by hills. The flames leaped up high, licking the sky's belly and the Great Spirit liked what he felt and saw, for three days later, there was a deluge and the land and the rivers were washed clean, and the sleeping spirit under the earth awakened, and the grass grew and the flowers bloomed and all the forest animals came back and the buffalo herds came again and there was much hunting and rejoicing.'

•For a moment, McCall was lost in nearly forgotten memories. Then he blinked and saw there was silence amongst the miners as they watched him. He drew a deep breath. 'It was a long time ago,' he mumbled.

'It sounds a great place to be,' someone muttered. 'Maybe that spirit would help us find gold!'

Some of the men laughed. McCall glared at them.

'If you go digging and polluting those hills, you'll never have anything but bad luck! I'm warning you!'

Silently he stalked away, too emotional to stay with them.

The young boy watched him go, hesitating as if he would have liked to talk with him further. But seeing the set of the scout's shoulders, he let well alone.

McCall tended to the horse the captain had loaned him. He was a good ride, but he preferred his own mount who knew his moods and needs.

Still, the old feller would be well rested and cared for when he returned to the detachment.

As he worked on the horse, he remembered his early childhood and the now dimmed face of his mother, the pretty Cheyenne girl who'd become William McCall's squaw wife. She had called him Little Buffalo because his father was known as Old Buffalo or Buff for short. She'd sung to him, given him the best pieces of meat to eat and wrapped him in a buffalo robe to sleep. He remembered on the infrequent visits of his father, how the big burly man with the grizzled beard had picked him up and tossed him high in the air, laughing at him when he squealed. Then there would be laughter and plenty of buffalo meat and presents for his mother, Moonwater, and sometimes there was a present for him, sugar candy from the white man's Store. Once Old Buffalo brought some tin soldiers.

But the memory of his mother

brought back the dreaded scene when the soldiers had ridden into the small Cheyenne village when the men were away hunting. They'd massacred all the old men, women and children. He'd been out gathering buffalo chips in a woven basket for his mother's fire when they'd struck. He'd crouched down under a bush and watched as his mother was dragged out from their tipi and bludgeoned to death. The soldier's face was printed indelibly on his mind. He remembered the bloodlust in the eyes, the scarred face where an Indian tomahawk had nearly killed him which had left a horrendous puckering of the face. He'd know him anywhere if he was still alive.

Then later, after months of being cared for by the remaining Cheyenne, his father had returned, but instead of being welcomed, he'd been attacked by a Cheyenne Quick Stinger and killed in revenge for the village massacre.

Then Buff, a ten year old boy, had panicked and run away from the village out into the wilderness. He'd nearly died until he'd stumbled on to a trail and was found by a caravan going west. He became a chuckwagon doughboy helping Cookie until he was old enough and big enough to break away. Then he joined the army as a scout with the vague idea of searching out the soldier who killed his father. At that time he had no idea just how many soldiers were in the white man's army.

But he still looked for that man.

Suddenly he was hit by elation as he remembered the Indian he'd killed. He found himself thanking the Great Spirit for allowing him to avenge his father. Maybe he would lead him to his mother's killer too?

Then he realized something else about himself. He was more Cheyenne than Scottish as he'd known his father to be. He didn't think as a white man even though for years he'd modelled himself on his father.

If there was going to be war between

the white men and the Indian tribes, which he was firmly convinced there would be, which side would he favour?

The answer came easy. He would ride with Chief Red Cloud.

3

The boy coming towards him looked like buzzard meat, thin and puny with a white haggard face and huge eyes that showed how frightened he was.

McCall judged him to be around fourteen, if that. His figure was small and his clothes looked two sizes too big for him. He wore a cloth cap with a peak. His hair was dark and curly; he might have been a good-looking kid if he'd had some meat on him.

McCall stopped what he was doing and stroked the horse's back leg, for he was a restive brute, as he watched him come close.

'Mister, can I talk to you?' The boy's voice quavered.

'Yeh, if you must. What's worrying you, boy?'

'It's just . . . my pa. That captain feller wants all the bodies to be buried together. He says it will be faster, but I want my pa to be buried separate, like.'

'You've got a spade, I expect. Dig a hole and bury him yourself!' McCall stood upright and stared at the kid who was wetting his dry lips with his tongue. He looked forlorn and helpless and McCall suddenly saw himself when he'd lost his own pa. He noted the boy's hands were white and unused to hard labour.

The boy looked up to him and he looked about to cry. 'Could you . . . . would you help me?'

'Hell! Didn't your pa ever put you to work? What's the matter with you? Have you consumption or something?'

The boy shook his head. 'I'm strong, mister. It's just that Pa sent me to school.'

'While he sweated his guts in a coal pit to keep you there?'

'He said the only way to get on was to be educated,' the kid replied defensively.

'Well, he sure didn't reckon you would be much help digging for gold in them there hills! He did you no favour, boy by not letting you flex those muscles you haven't got!'

The boy turned away and muttered something over his shoulder.

'What's that you say?'

'I said go to hell! I'll bury him myself!'

'What's so goddamn special about him that he has to have a burial on his lonesome?'

'He was my pa, that's what!' The boy stamped away. McCall watched him go, then swore heartily and the horse did some fancy steps in alarm. 'Whoa there, you spring-loaded dog's leg! Save your legs for some real riding!'

Then he was away and following the boy to one of the wagons where the boy was rummaging through the piled-up gear to find a spade. The body of a man was lying by the wagon.

'You got another spade?' called McCall.

The boy raised his head from the wagon and his face split into a smile. McCall thought he didn't look so much like a starving waif.

'You'll help me?'

'What the hell d'you think I want the spade for? I don't dig holes for fun!'

After the job was over and the body buried, the lad took off his cap and stood for a few minutes with eyes shut and lips moving soundlessly. Then his eyes flipped open and he looked straight at McCall.

'Someday, I reckon I'll have my revenge on those Indians. I hate all Indians now and I always will!'

McCall nodded. 'I understand how you feel, boy.'

'Did an Indian kill your pa?'

'Yes, but I don't talk about it.' He turned away. A hand grasped his arm.

'Mister, would you ride with me? I've never driven a team before.'

McCall stifled an oath. 'You don't expect me to wet-nurse you, boy? What the hell's your name, anyway?'

'I'm Charlie . . . Charlie Norris. My pa was Ned.'

'Have you any kin you can go back to, Charlie?'

Charlie shook his head. 'There was only me and Pa after Ma died. It was hard and Pa always dreamed of making it rich. That's why he took a chance and sold everything to come out here.'

'But you'll have to go back, Charlie. The army won't let you go further into the territory.'

'But the other fellers are going!'

McCall shook his head. 'Only to Piney Ridge where we're setting up camp before we start building a set of forts all the way to the Black Hills.'

'Well, I can help build! I can work from fort to fort until we get there. I'm strong. Surely there's something I can do. I can't go back, mister. I've nothing to go back for!'

McCall looked at the agonized face and the jaw that might be stubborn if there was more flesh on it. Somehow

32

the boy looked older. He sighed inwardly.

'I'll have to talk to the colonel once we get back to the others. I'm warning you, Charlie, he'll think you're too young to work in the wilderness. We're expecting trouble, you know. There will be Indian attacks for sure. We'll be lucky if one fort is built.'

'I don't care. I want to go along and then, someday, I might get to them there hills and find me a pot of gold!'

McCall laughed and shook his head. 'You're a dreamer, Charlie boy, but I like your spirit.'

'Will you ride with me?'

McCall considered. He didn't reckon that he would be an army scout much longer. He could do as he liked and if Captain Platte didn't like it, he could shove himself up his own ass.

'I'll ride with you until you get the knack of it. Four horses isn't much harder to control than two.'

He looked at the boy's puny arms

and knew he was telling lies. This boy wouldn't get far without help.

* * *

The captain was impatient. 'If those bodies are buried, let's get on and make rendezvous with the colonel. I don't want those Stingers back with reinforcements, so let's ride!'

He looked down his nose when McCall explained about riding with the boy.

'You're not here to do any wet-nursing, McCall. One of those miners could drive the boy's wagon. Put someone else on to it!'

'With all due respect, sir, the boy doesn't want any of the miners to take over his wagon.'

'Does he think he might lose it?'

McCall nodded. 'Between you and me, sir, they look a cut-throat lot.'

'Well, we'll knock 'em into shape when they come to cutting down timber and hacking out virgin land. There'll be

34

no time for skullduggery. Anyhow, the boy should go back to Fort Laramie with the men who are going back.'

'Sir, I think he wants to go on and help build the camp.'

'Does he, by God! He's a bit of a whippersnapper, isn't he? Maybe he could do the cooking if he wants to help.'

'I'll put it to him, sir.'

'You do that. Tell him I give him permission to travel on if he cooks, and God help him if he can't cook! And you, McCall, stop this assing about and get out there and do the job you're paid for!'

Charlie grinned when he told him of the captain's decision.

'Don't get your hopes up too high, Charlie. You've got to convince the colonel.'

'Oh, I can cook. Tonight I'll dish up the captain's grub and he can tell the colonel what a good cook I am. By the way, I can't keep calling you mister. What should I call you?'

'I'm McCall.'

'But you must have another name?'

McCall shrugged. 'My mother called me Little Buffalo and my pa called me Buff so I guess I'm Buff.'

Charlie looked shocked and several expressions crossed his face.

'What you looking like that for?' McCall was angry.

'Why . . . I didn't realize . . . ' his voice tailed away.

'You mean you don't like the idea of me being part Indian?'

Charlie swallowed. 'I didn't say that.'

'You looked it! I can't help what I am. My mother was Cheyenne and I'm proud of it. If you don't like it, I'll get on my way and you can find someone else to drive for you!'

He turned to go and the boy caught his arm.

'Don't go! It was just the shock of knowing. It doesn't make any difference to you and me.'

'You said you would hate all Indians for ever!'

'Not you. You're different. I want us to be friends, Buff.' He held out his hand.

McCall gripped it, aware of how pitifully weak it was. Hell! He couldn't turn his back on this kid! It was obvious the boy needed a friend.

'Right! We're friends and we won't talk about this any more. Is it a deal?'

The boy's face split into a smile. His eyes danced and McCall was startled to see they were a clear bright blue. He was an intriguing little cuss, all right.

'It's a deal!'

McCall sorted out the rig and they lined up behind the other wagons with the captain and half his men leading the way. The rest followed with Sergeant Button behind.

It was slow travelling and when the wagons were rolling well, McCall handed over the reins to Charlie.

'Just hold the reins firm, Charlie, don't let them slacken and the leaders will follow the wagon in front. Right?'

Unaccountably the boy looked nervous. 'You're not leaving me?'

'I'll be back. I'm just taking a look-see. There's rocks ahead and a gulley and I've got a job to do, so stiffen that spine of yours and remember you're not a kid any more!'

He untied his horse, mounted and then, with a last look at Charlie, galloped away to confer with Captain Platte before he rode ahead and surveyed the land for signs of Indians or other travellers moving ahead.

The rolling hills were pine-covered and he could see snailtrails where rivers ran. He watched for buzzards sweeping the skies, tell-tale signs of death and slaughter.

Everywhere he looked was quiet. There were no disturbances of birds or hazy smoke lifting high into the sky. He felt a sudden rush of freedom. This was how it should be, a peaceful existence, not bound by civilization's needs. He understood why the Sioux and the other tribes were fighting to save their untrammelled way of life.

Suddenly the white men were the marauders, the polluters, the evil darkness that was smothering the earth and growing stronger year by year.

As he rode, he had a vision in his mind's eye of the Black Hills' agony as more and more men would come to plunder its riches, dig holes in the sacred ground, desecrate the sacred places and let the demon of despair rule where once the Great Spirit ruled.

There came upon him a great sadness, and he vowed that when he finally reached those hills again, he would face the east and pray to the Great Spirit to give him the courage to fight and die for them.

He had to honour his true beliefs.

When he returned to the wagon train and the detail he was a changed man. He wasn't an army scout with an army scout's loyalty to the army which paid him. He was his own man.

But there was a job to be done. He

and Fish Eye were responsible for early warnings of attack and disruption. He must at least maintain his duty until the first work camp was completed.

Colonel Carrington's disapproval was taken out on Captain Platte for bringing the wagon train along with the troops. 'What in hell were you thinking about, Captain? Godalmighty! We've got enough trouble without looking out for these blasted no-hopers! You should have sent them back . . . all of them. Do you hear? You took too much on yourself, Captain and it will go down on your record!'

'But Colonel, they were determined! Two men have turned back. God knows whether they'll reach Fort Laramie. I couldn't send troops with them . . . '

'I should damn well think not! We need every able-bodied man on two legs to get this project under way! I suppose they can all use an axe?'

'Yes, they're all used to hard labour, excepting for the kid, of course.'

'Kid? What kid?'

Captain Platte coughed. 'Er . . . the kid who lost his old man. He was determined to come along.'

'Determined? You mean to tell me you allowed a kid to overrule you? What kind of an officer are you?' The captain reddened.

'Sir . . . '

'Damn my eyes! I wonder what the powers that be expect me to do with incy-mincy fellers like you on the frontier? You'll be turning Indian-lover next!'

'Sir, I'd like it to be put on record, that I firmly think we should honour our commitments to the Indians. There's been too many promises made and broken . . . '

'You're actually taking those heathens' side?'

'They've got rights, sir.'

'Rights? Don't talk to me about Indian rights! You're a fool, Platte. God put that gold into those hills for the white man to find! The damned Indians don't know the value of gold!

It would be a sin to leave it in the ground. Why, man, everyone with guts who goes out there when the time is right will come away with a fortune!'

'The hills are on the land ceded to them,' said Platte doggedly.

'To hell with that! Nobody suspected gold until Custer found traces. For God's sake, Platte, revise your thinking or I'll have to get a replacement for you!'

'I shall do my duty, sir, but it doesn't mean I approve!'

Colonel Carrington stared him up and down. 'I believe you mean every word you said.' He took a deep breath and then softly with a hidden menace in his voice. 'Get out of my sight, Platte and send Lieutenant Saunders to me.'

'Yes, sir!' Captain Platte saluted and turned stiffly to walk away, knowing full well that he'd just bungled any chance of promotion.

He shrugged. Well, let the old pig do his worst! It would be far better to get a desk job in Washington and get noticed. His father would grease a few palms and maybe one day he would give the colonel his comeuppance!

He was in a thoroughly bad temper when he sent his batman to tell Saunders that the old dick was on the prod and to take care and give all the right answers.

He sought out Buff McCall who was sitting with Fish Eye around their own fire. McCall was picking his teeth. The dried jerky was tougher than usual and the biscuits had been half raw. He was considering asking the army cook if the kid in the wagon train could help him sling the hash. Cookie was touchy about his cooking. He'd have to be careful how he tackled the subject.

Both he and Fish Eye sat up hurriedly when Platte approached. Both were ready and expecting an order to saddle up and take a ride.

Platte waved a hand. 'Don't get up, boys. Just want a chinwag.'

They all settled around the small fire. Fish Eye produced a bottle of red eye.

'You want a swig, Captain?'

Platte shook his head. 'You've got to have steel guts for that, Fish Eye. You go ahead and give yourself an ulcer. I'll miss out.'

Fish Eye lifted his shoulders. 'Makes life worth living. You want a shot, McCall?'

'Yeh, why not?' He downed a slug that would have made a mule bug-eyed. Platte watched appreciatively.

'How the hell you scouts can stomach that stuff, I'll never know.'

'Brought up on it like mother's milk,' Fish Eye intoned, taking the bottle from McCall and drinking until he belched. He sighed deeply and corked the bottle. 'Now I can listen comfortably while you say what you come to say.' He looked at Platte owlishly.

McCall looked Platte over. Maybe Fish Eye had seen something he'd missed. 'What is it, Captain?' Now when he thought about it, the man seemed upset.

'Look, I want you to know how I

stand on this expedition. I know you two will have your ears to the ground and know how things stand. I even guess that when you go off scouting you might even rendezvous with the Sioux. If you do, it's none of my business. All I want to know is, how far off are we to the big explosion?'

Fish Eye tensed and looked far into space, suddenly not with them any more.

Platte looked from him to McCall. 'Well?'

'It's hard to say, Captain. The young hotheads talk about all the five nations sending their best braves to defend the hills. The older ones, the chiefs and medicine men are for holding off and talking again with the government and trying to come to some agreement. The young ones don't want to wait. They see their lands being taken from them. Already the white men have decimated the buffalo herds and they must hunt farther afield than ever. They see their families starving and being herded into the designated reservations. The red men have always been free men. They're proud and don't want to be told where to live and what to do by strangers who have come to their land and taken it from them. It is not right.'

He stopped to draw breath. He wasn't a man for making speeches, but he couldn't have stopped himself. It suddenly meant so much to him.

'I agree with you, McCall. I want you to know that.'

'Then why are you here and not in Washington opening your mouth and saying what you think?'

'Because I'm a coward, McCall, and there are too many men who expect to make fortunes out in this new West.' He spoke sadly. 'I only hope this camp building isn't going to be a failure. If it is . . . ' he paused, 'then a lot of good brave men will die!'

McCall grunted. 'We'll have to fight all the way to Piney Ridge. If I were you, Captain, I would recommend that the Gatling gun should be manned at all times, and it would be best if it brought up the rear of the wagon train. That way, it could be in use before the wagons could be positioned in a circle.'

'Hmm, I see your point. You're part Cheyenne. Don't you think you're betraying them by being a scout?' Platte looked at McCall with mounting interest.

'In this instance, Captain, we're fighting the Sioux. The Cheyenne will go along with them because they are affiliated and they have the same interest in the Black Hills as do other tribes. But I have no loyalty to the Cheyenne.'

'Why?'

'They killed my father when I was a child. Now if you will excuse me, I'll go check the horses.'

He swung easily to his feet in one easy movement and walked away, leaving Captain Platte to watch him go, thinking what a complex man he was.

Fish Eye returned from wherever he'd been in his own private place.

'He's a good man, Captain but mixed up. What d'you expect when you've got the blood of two different cultures warring in your veins?'

'You think he can be trusted?'

'As much as you can trust anyone, Captain.'

The captain grunted. 'I'll surely be glad when we reach Piney Ridge!' He stalked away.

Fish Eye followed his progress, whispering softly, '*If* we reach Piney Ridge!'

McCall sought out the miners who sat in their own group. He missed the boy amongst them.

'Where's Charlie? He doesn't want to be wandering away on his own.' He looked around at them all.

They were a mixed bag, all hard fit men with well-developed muscles from hard graft in the mines. None of them looked like leaders or thinkers. All good men to take orders. They would be invaluable at the camp, but now?

'How many of you have a gun?'

They looked at each other, then one of them spoke for the rest.

'We all have guns but we're miners, not gunnies. Anyway, we're only three days from Piney Ridge and the soldiers are the ones to defend us if it's necessary. Me, I don't believe the Indians will attack again. After all, they must have learned a lesson, losing all them braves. No, they'll lick their wounds . . .'

'You're a fool! If you think that way, you'll be shot in the back. Now where's that boy?'

They all shrugged, all indifferent to a boy who'd just lost his father. Not one of them had offered to look out for the youth. The cold-hearted self-centred bastards, McCall thought contemptuously.

'We're not his keepers,' someone called sullenly. 'We've enough to do

49

to look out for ourselves.'

'But you expect the troopers to look out for you!'

'It's their right, if they expect us to work on that camp! I suppose they're going to pay us?'

'Pay you? Like hell they will! You're in forbidden territory as it is. You shouldn't be here. You should have gone back to Fort Laramie with the others!'

The miners began to look angry and stared at each other.

'I think we should have a word with that jumped-up colonel. I'm not sweating my guts felling trees for nothing!' someone in the back of the bunch roared.

'You do that, mister, and you might find yourself left behind to fight the Sioux yourself!'

The men looked uneasy.

'Maybe we should have gone back . . . '

'What? After spending all we had on tools and grub?'

'I didn't think it was going to be risky . . . '

'We could lose our scalp-locks!'

'Stop panicking! Those damned officers might want to keep the diggings to themselves! Keep the troopers busy when they're not riding out looking for trouble! I say we should stay and get in there and stake a claim. After all, those hills are only hills. Who in his right mind would lay his life down for a range of pine-covered hills? Those Indians could find another range to kowtow to!'

McCall left them in disgust. They would argue amongst themselves for hours. But one thing was sure, the ignorant sons of bitches would learn they were very wrong.

He found Charlie sitting under a tree staring into space.

'You missing your pa?'

The boy nodded but said nothing. He was white-faced and shrunken into himself.

'He was a good pa, was he?'

51

'Yeh. A bit rough. Never said much but he was kind and he was always there for me.'

'Protect you too much, I guess.'

The boy moved uncomfortably. 'He wanted me to better myself. Know about books and such. Didn't think too much about himself being just a rough miner.'

'You'll get over it, kid. Life has to go on.'

'I've been wondering what I should do.'

'Well, you can't go back on your own and those friends of yours are determined to go ahead.'

'They're not my friends! Pa only teamed up with them because they all had the same goal in mind. They all talked about gold. My pa did too. Thought it was the one chance of making it rich.'

'And now you're not so sure?'

'There's things you don't know.'

'What things?'

The boy turned away, hiding his

expression from the scout. 'Just things
. . . private things.'

'If you can't talk about them, I can't
help you.'

'Would you help me?'

'If I knew how I could help you.
Yes.'

There was a long silence and then
Charlie said softly, 'Someday, if we
survive and we get to the Black Hills,
I'll tell you.'

'Please yourself. Now let's get back
to the others and don't go off on your
own again. There could be someone
out there watching us even now.'

The boy turned pale. McCall sighed
inwardly. He wished the poor little
belter had a bit more spunk. He should
have been a girl . . .

The boy shivered. 'I'll remember.
Thanks for the warning.'

'Have you met our dough puncher
yet?'

Charlie shook his head. 'I took my
fixin's and coffee and went and sat by
myself.'

'You get in good with him, kid, and he'll build up that skinny body of yours. You'll get the leavin's.'

The boy pulled a face. 'He's a rotten cook!'

'Nevertheless, he'll keep your belly filled and if you help him, scrub his pans and run after him, he'll see you right. Billy Joe might be rough and ready but he's a good man.'

'Will you introduce me?'

'Yeh, if you're a bit scary about bellying up to him.'

So McCall introduced Charlie to the burly bald-headed Billy Joe who scratched his bearded chin, looked him up and down and spat at Charlie's feet.

'You want for to work for me?' Then he looked at McCall. 'What about Dryballed Harry? Will he object?'

'He won't know if you don't tell him. How many times does he visit the chuck wagon?'

'Yeh, you're right. As long as his tin plate's full, he don't care. Now Captain

54

Platte be different. He comes looking to see I ain't putting poison in that there stew.'

'You can always send Charlie off somewhere when you see him coming.'

Billy Joe scratched his head. 'Ay dear . . . I don' know . . . '

'Aw, come on, Billy Joe, none of them other coal diggin' bastards are willing to look out for him!'

'Look out for him? Chre-ist! He'd only be a humble pot walloper! You look out for him!'

'Now you know I can't do that. I'm here and there and all over along with Fish Eye. Come on, Billy Joe, do something you can be proud of. Look after this kid.'

Charlie turned away, head bent.

'Look, I can look after myself! I don't need to be where I'm not wanted! I'll get back to my wagon, and in future, I don't need anyone to help me with the horses!'

He began to run and McCall caught him by the shoulder and shook him.

'Look, you little devil, I'm trying to do my best for you! Billy Joe's all mouth. He'll come round. I know he will.'

Charlie stuck out his chin and glared at McCall, and again, McCall wondered just how young the kid was. There was no sign of fluff on his chin. A bit of a late starter, he reckoned.

'Who the hell d'you think you are? I've told you I can look out for myself!'

McCall didn't answer but dragged him back to Billy Joe.

'You look out for him, Billy Joe, and don't say another word and next time I'm out I'll bring in some fresh meat. A deal?'

Billy Joe laughed. 'I thought you were never going to say! It's a deal!'

McCall was grinning when he walked away, thinking, the sly old fox! He was for looking out for the kid all the time, but was dragging his heels because he knew that McCall would finally bribe him with talk of fresh meat. They'd had private transactions before and it always came down to McCall hunting for the pot.

The boy looked after him. 'Hey! What about me?'

McCall turned, pointing a finger. 'You do your part, and let me go hunt meat! I'll be back.'

For a long moment the boy watched him go and then turned to Billy Joe.

'Right! What d'do you want me to do?'

'D'you know how to make dough?'

Charlie nodded. 'Yeh, used to do it for Pa and I can make panbread and I know how to make an Indian oven with hot stones. Anything else?'

Billy Joe looked impressed.

'You know a lot for a little sprig of a kid. What else you know?'

'I know how to make that pulque drink the Indians are so fond of and cider when there's apples around.'

'Can you now? Maybe we're going to get on better than I thought.'

'I'll try my best.'

'Right. Well, you see that pile of

turnips? Just get a sharp knife and peel 'em ready for the pot. We're going to make a mighty big stew.'

Charlie grimaced and reluctantly went to the big box on the side of the wagon where the cutting tools were kept. He chose what he wanted and got a start.

McCall spent the night on watch taking it in turns with Fish Eye to patrol the perimeter of the makeshift camp. They would be moving out at dawn, but he wanted to be sure that the Sioux were not waiting for a dawn attack.

He saw four troopers on guard around the tents, but they were not field men. The only time they would sense an Indian nearby would be when an arrow blasted through them or a gunshot blew them away.

He and Fish Eye were going to have to double up on guard duties from now on until they got to Piney Ridge . . . if they got there.

He patrolled further and further out

from the camp. He could see it silent and quiet in the moonlight, the only movement the troopers on guard. He saw how vulnerable they were. He'd have a word with Captain Platte in the morning that from now onwards there would be no smoking on duty and that they must choose alternative cover and learn to move like an Indian, even if they were convinced they were not being observed.

It was when he was making his last round before returning to Fish Eye that he saw the figures standing motionless on a ridge overlooking the camp.

He dismounted and left his horse under a stand of trees. He'd been careful to follow the line of the trees and so was not seen from above. So, from moving from bush to bush, he climbed higher until he was within two hundred yards of the observers.

He watched for a while, noting the warpaint, the lances and the old out-of-date guns they carried. They handled them clumsily as if not really happy with them. Probably ancient buffalo hunter weapons, swapped for furs from some trader. They wouldn't be cleaned and oiled, and maybe they would blow up when fired.

He watched them without emotion. They were Sioux and he had no blood ties with them. He neither liked nor hated them. All he wanted was to know their intentions and how many more of them there were.

They were watchers, so he moved on over the ridge and was shocked when he saw the size of the hunting party waiting for the dawn attack.

He slithered away, back down the slope, past the watchers and down to his horse. Thank God it was his own horse trained to stand still and not to nicker at his approach. He took the reins and, instead of riding away, walked and made a wide detour so that he came within the camp from the other side and out of sight of the men on the rim.

He startled Fish Eye who'd been

dozing and was ready to take to his horse and take over.

'For the love of the Great Spirit, don't creep up on me like that. If it hadn't been for your smell, I'd have put my knife in you!'

McCall put a warning hand on his shoulder. 'Don't move. Listen. We got company back there, and they'll be calling at dawn. Can you get under canvas and rouse the men without being seen? I'd do it myself but I want to get to the colonel and the captain. Look along the ridge there and you'll see the advance guard. Once they see the troops break out for breakfast, they're going to signal the attack.'

Fish Eye saw the situation as it was at a glance.

'I'll move like a sidewinder. I'll be in and out of that row of tents like a flash of lightning. They'll be ready with weapons cocked and waiting for orders to leave the tents on the colonel's orders. Sergeant Billy Button will know what to do.'

'That's it. You've got it, Fish Eye. Let those bastards up there think the camp is still sleeping.'

McCall slipped away and, keeping to the shadows, came upon the two tents occupied by the officers. He slid inside one and suddenly there was a muffled shout.

'Who the hell's that?' There was a movement as if someone groped for a candle. McCall gripped the colonel's wrist.

'It's McCall, sir. Don't light up. There's a hunting party out there, waiting for dawn. Fish Eye's warning the men. They're going to be ready and waiting for your orders, sir.'

'They'll not leave the tents?'

'No sir. The idea is to let 'em think the camp is still sleeping.'

'What about the guards?'

'They know nothing, sir. We thought it best that way, so they won't do anything different from usual.'

The colonel grunted. 'They could get themselves killed.'

'It's one of the hazards of being a soldier, sir.'

'You're a cold-blooded swine, McCall. You've eaten and drunk with those men, but then of course you're part Cheyenne and can't be expected to think like a white man!'

McCall balled his fists. He would have liked to feel the colonel's nose crunch under one of them.

'Yes sir. I'll go and warn the captain, sir.' He slid away before the colonel could reply.

Captain Platte was cool and business-like. He'd experienced situations like this before.

'Thank you, McCall. I'll not forget this. Can you warn the miners? I expect they have weapons of their own. I'll have to get to the gun crew. It's a good job they sleep next to the big gun.'

'Yes sir. I'll go now then, and see to the miners.'

He was away and slithering and belly-hopping under the shadow of tents and wagons. Soon they were all waiting.

He found Charlie bemused and frightened, when he shook him awake.

'What's going on?'

'The camp's under attack.'

'I don't hear anything.'

'You will when dawn comes.'

Charlie sat up with a jerk. 'Hell! D'you mean those varmints have come back?'

'Them or another hunting party. It could be a revenge attack. Have you got a gun?'

Charlie swallowed. 'Pa had an old shotgun. It's under the driver's seat.'

'Then get to it and load up. You do know how to use it?'

'Yeh, I suppose so.'

'Suppose so? Goddammit! Either you do or you don't!'

'I think I can.'

'Here, give it to me. I'll see to it, and for God's sake, don't tell me you don't know where the extra ammunition is!'

'Oh no, I know where that is. There's

a box under the seat with the gun.'

McCall gave a sigh of relief. They were going to need every bit of ammunition before the next few hours passed.

He loaded up and waited with the boy. He couldn't leave him.

4

Sub-chief Broken Nose silently joined the watchers on the rim looking down on the sleeping camp. For a long moment he watched as the sentries smoked their cigarettes and moved around the tents, sometimes unseen as they passed the circle of wagons.

'They sleep soundly,' he muttered. 'May the dogs sleep soundly for ever!' He looked at the sky where the first streaks of the false dawn were coming through racing clouds. 'It will be a good day for the Sioux! We will show those white men in Washington that they cannot make the red men promises they don't keep! Today will be a warning.'

One of the painted warriers asked the question they all wanted to know.

'When will it be, Broken Nose?'

Again Broken Nose looked at the sky and turned to the east, raising his hands and in a low tone asked a blessing of the Great Spirit.

There was a general murmur as his braves listened to the prayer. Then taking a deep breath, and waving his lance, he imitated the call of the plover, a long drawn out wail that galvanized the warriors waiting below.

Up they came, scrambling like goats, silent as snakes, and yelling the war cry of the Sioux when they reached the summit, they poured down the embankment to the camp below, guns roaring. Firebrands were thrown at tents and some warriors were intent on slaughtering sleeping men now thrown into panic.

But it didn't happen like that. The tent flaps opened and a volley of bullets cut a swathe through the advancing pack. Then, horror of horrors, the spitting dragon that was the white man's god started its rattle and the Gatling gun mounted on a wagon spat bullets in a lethal wave of destruction. Its mighty snub nose moved from side to side as a soldier worked the handle that motivated the monster.

Broken Nose paused to take aim at the trooper manipulating the gun and watched him pitch over and down from the wagon. There was a pause but another took his place and the killing went on, leaving Broken Nose suddenly feeling sick and frightened.

He looked about him; already there were braves who were lying still and bloody among the troopers who had fallen. He remembered Red Cloud's words. 'We want to harass them, not to get our own braves killed. We must wait to see if the men in Washington change their minds about the Black Hills. It is only *then* that we go to war and I ask for the lives of the brave Sioux!'

Red Cloud was not going to be impressed by this day's work. He'd totally overlooked the Gatling gun, for it had been covered by tarpaulin and he'd figured, as he'd watched the army detail set out from Fort Laramie, that the wagon only carried supplies.

McCall in Charlie's wagon looked across at him when the yelling began.

'Don't crap yourself, kid. Keep cool and wait until you see the whites of their eyes before you shoot. You can't miss then.' Charlie gulped and nodded, fully aware that a full bladder had streamed down a leg in a hot gush. Then his ears rang as McCall's rifle exploded and a bloodcurdling shriek and the thump of a hurtling body proclaimed one down and many more to come.

Then suddenly he was wide-eyed and looking at a copper-coloured and half naked figure with grotesque face-paint, yelling like a fanatic. The sight paralysed him. To Charlie it was as if he was coming in slow motion, hand raised to throw his lance, a howling demon whose eyes spouted hate.

'Shoot, you goddamn fool!'

Charlie was aware of McCall beside him firing with cool precision into a bunch of whirling bodies. He was also vaguely aware of McCall's order.

It took all his will and strength to pull the trigger on the clumsy old gun. It exploded, knocking him backwards and he knew he would have a thumping bruise on his shoulder, if he lived to examine it later.

He scrambled to his feet, half expecting the Indian would be upon him to lift his hair. He saw the crumpled heap on the ground, blood welling from a ghastly great hole in the chest.

He wanted to be sick, but hadn't the time. His hands trembling, he loaded up and when McCall paused to reload, he aimed the shotgun and fired and watched the devastation a shotgun can make.

But now the Indians were being more cautious. There was the urgent cry of the plover and Charlie was surprised to see the remnants of the bunch dropping back. It surely wasn't because he'd used the shotgun? Vaguely he'd been aware of the spitting Gatling amidst the rifle fire.

McCall wiped his perspiring face. 'I think the tide's turned.' Then he looked sideways at Charlie. 'What happened to you? I thought you were going to let him scalp you without fighting back.'

Charlie shook his head. 'I was shit-scared, Buff. I shot him in response to your shout. If it hadn't been for that, I should be dead now.'

'You're a queer little devil, Charlie. You'd never make a soldier. Your best bet would be to go back east and get a job in a store or something. You're not cut out for this kind of life.'

He didn't wait for Charlie's reaction to this but climbed carefully from the wagon, looking around for stray invaders. He was surprised to see that they were gone.

The troopers were already reloading and cleaning weapons, for there might be a second wave of attackers. The remaining miners looked dazed and frightened. Billy Joe was handing out hard tack rations to those who passed by. Horses were fed and got ready and there were signs that the tents that remained were coming down and that the detachment was getting ready to move out as soon as possible.

McCall reported to Colonel Carrington and saluted.

'Where the hell have you been, McCall? I expected to see some action from you. Or couldn't you bring yourself to kill a Sioux?'

'The Sioux are nothing to me, sir. I was defending the rear,' he replied woodenly, his insides churning with hatred for this arrogant swine.

'You should have been with Sergeant Button. He's dead. Corporal Saunders had to take over.'

'Sir, with all respect, I'm hired by the army but I am not part of it. I was helping to defend the miners.'

'That kid, I expect. You seem to have an unhealthy liking for him, haven't you, McCall?'

That was when McCall hit him.

Colonel Carrington sprawled on the ground, his face twisting with rage as he fingered his bruised chin. McCall's knuckles stung but it was nothing compared to the exultation he felt. The colonel had had it coming.

'How dare you! I'll have you shot, you halfbreed bastard! Where's Captain Platte?' he shouted to a nearby soldier who was standing as if mesmerized. The man didn't answer but sped away.

'I want this man taken prisoner!' Carrington bawled to anyone near enough to hear.

'Like hell you will!' McCall dragged him to his feet and planted another punch on the jaw. Carrington's legs buckled like jelly and, as the onlookers watched in disbelief, he ran behind the tents to where his horse was tethered. With a coolness he would never have believed of himself he saddled up and rode away.

He thought of Charlie. A pity he hadn't had the time to say goodbye. He was a taking little runt. He hoped

Billy Joe would look after him.

The anger and bitterness rode with him. It had been yeasting inside him for a long time. Today, after the tension of the Indian attack, he had just boiled over. If he had stayed, he would surely have backshot the Indian-hating son of a bitch.

He rode ahead of the detachment, instinctively looking out for signs of the Sioux. He came upon a stream, dismounted and drank alongside his horse. He stared at himself in the clear water.

He saw an Indian-dark face, moody and brooding. His eyes were blue, the only indication of his white father. Inside himself, he knew he sometimes thought as a white man, and sometimes he was a free spirit like his mother's people. He felt as if he was two persons inside one body. The blood of both tugged him in different directions.

But now, he felt the call of the wild. He was sick of the arrogance of the white men and the harsh cruelty he'd seen over the years. The white men regarded the Indians as little more than animals with no rights, no feelings and no pride. He was finished with them.

He took off his army issue hat and threw it away, and along with it the deerskin jerkin he wore. Slowly he stripped, baring his chest and tossing away the stinking army shirt. He gazed into the water. Already he was looking more like what he should be. He felt his spirits rise.

Then off came the moccasins and the army pants and he stood tall and straight and proud.

He plunged into the river, feeling the hard bite of crystal cold water. He allowed it to purge him of the stench of the white man. He felt revitalized and reborn. From now on he would regard himself as Cheyenne and fight for the Black Hills alongside the united tribes when the time came to fight. He would contact Red Cloud and offer his allegiance.

He clambered out of the water,

which streamed from him. He shook his wet head and dried himself roughly on the shirt. Then he tore his jerkin, fashioned himself a breech-clout and reached for his moccasins.

The gentle breeze cooled his skin. He saw there were more differences than he'd realized; his skin was lighter than an Indian's. It betrayed his parentage. Taking up some mud from the bank of the stream he daubed himself all over and as far as he could reach. It would have to do until he got an all-over tan from the sun.

Then, picking up his army issue rifle and hand-gun in its holster, he strapped on his belt and the bandolier filled with bullets.

He contemplated leaving his horse's saddle behind, but thought that might be carrying things too far. Indeed, he needed the panniers for where he was heading.

For two days he watched the slow moving detachment as it kept pace with the wagons. He also saw the accompanying Sioux who were spying from a safe distance. They were regarding the Gatling gun mounted on the last wagon with awe. It was a deterrent not to be ignored.

At last the wagon train reached Piney Ridge. It was a long-time derelict settlement, that had housed a group of timberhawks. The land had been cleared of timber and, because it had become unprofitable, the loggers had moved on. Now it would serve a useful purpose once the new cabins and lookouts were built. There would be much hauling of logs and the miners' wagons would be useful alongside the army issue.

The camp would be situated at the top of a hill with the stream flowing below.

All hands were soon at work, dragging supplies, setting up temporary quarters, organizing a camp kitchen and doing all the sundry jobs needed to build a permanent camp.

McCall watched the men start work.

He wanted to see that Charlie was all right before he went to seek Red Cloud. He glimpsed the boy working alongside Billy Joe. He didn't look too happy and McCall thought he looked thin and drawn.

He turned to go and then hesitated. He would probably never see the boy again. Something about the boy bothered him. It didn't seem right to ride away without explanation.

He would wait and when the lad wandered away into the bush as he was prone to do, he would speak with him. He felt better in his mind at his decision.

Later, he watched the men cluster round the makeshift cookhouse and take their tin plates of stew. It smelled good and made his guts churn a little. He watched Billy Joe and Charlie doling out steaming plates and pouring coffee until they were beaded with sweat.

He noticed too that the soldiers congregated away from the miners.

There was no real camaraderie between them.

Then suddenly there was a mighty roar. Tin plates went flying and a band of soldiers gathered round Billy Joe and Charlie.

'You stink, Billy Joe, and you've got the kid stinking too!'

'When you gonna wash, Billie Joe? Or do you scrape off the muck and add it to the stew?'

'What about dunking 'em in the river, boys? We could do 'em a favour and scrub their backs!'

There was a great peal of laughter as the men joshed Billy Joe. Charlie cowered back and looked frightened. But Billy Joe lashed out. He was angry. He was never one to take a joke.

He fisted a punch and sent the main joker sprawling. Then the mood turned ugly and McCall watched as they seized Billy Joe and Charlie and hauled them to the river's edge, both struggling helplessly.

The miners stood by laughing. Billy

Joe was a soldier and nothing to do with them, and as for Charlie, he was just a kid and not worth fighting over.

The soldiers stripped Billy Joe naked and threw him into the water, then two jumped in and dunked him several times.

Then it was Charlie's turn and his screams turned McCall's blood cold. Anger bit deeply and he was just cocking his rifle when suddenly the whole mob went silent. McCall looked at Charlie standing shivering in mid stream, hands across a white slender body, and he too gasped and stood silent, too stunned at what he saw.

Then a great howling went up and the watching men turned into woman-starved animals.

'Chre-ist! The kid's a woman!'

'Let's be at her!'

'Hold on, boys, We gotta play fair. How we decide who's gonna be first?'

'We auction her. I'll give a week's wages!'

'Hell! I'll double that!'

'Who'll hold the dough?'

'We'll let Corporal Saunders handle it. We can use it for booze later on. We'll need it,' the man grinned lasciviously.

'We still have to fix a list. I say we should get in line.'

'What's the matter, Stevens? Have you ants in your pants?'

They all laughed uproariously, drunk on the sight they were beholding.

Charlie, at first paralysed by shock and the manhandling looked both ways, up and down the river. It ran swiftly and downriver was a faint roar as it went over unseen falls.

Suddenly she took a deep breath and dived and allowed the water to carry her along before surfacing. It was one of the good things her father had taught her. She could hold her own in the river. She swam like a fish.

There was a great shout and several of the soldiers plunged after her. It was then that McCall fired above the heads of the group.

They stopped and stared at him. They could hardly believe their eyes to see their scout, stripped and all but naked and daubed in red clay.

'You bastards. Let her go. The first man who moves will get a bullet in the guts!'

He crouched on the other side of the river, rifle cocked and waited until he judged Charlie to be well down the river. Then standing, he sent a volley over their heads and ran.

Several shots whined past his ear but he was a swiftly moving target and the sun was in their eyes. He wasn't worried about the soldiers but he was bothered about drawing the attention of the Sioux who would be watching all that had occurred. He must find Charlie before the Sioux fished her out of the river.

He raced ahead, dodging bushes and leaping boulders that were strewn in his path. Then far ahead in the water, he saw the bobbing head and arms flailing the cascade as she was swept nearer the falls.

He saw an outlying pine trunk, long dead and precariously balancing over the water. With a mighty effort he jumped out on to it, praying his weight wouldn't snap the rottenness of it.

He watched her float past and then he dived in. With powerful strokes he chased her until he felt the relentless pull of the grey-brown water.

Then he stretched out his hand and entwined his fingers into her short curly hair which was plastered like a cap to her skull. At once their bodies came together and he clung to her just as they raced over the edge of the falls.

He felt her bury her head into his chest as they hurtled downwards amidst the angry white water, and then down, down, down as they plunged and swirled into the roar of an unknown underworld.

McCall was gasping and choking for

air as he surfaced. Charlie was a dead weight in his arms and as he fought to get out of the current he thought she was dead.

Her face was waxen, her lips blue.

He thrashed the water and suddenly found one foot touched the sandy bed of the river. He moved like a drunken man as he waded, coughing and fighting for breath as he hauled her ashore.

Then he collapsed with her in his arms.

He wanted to sleep. He had an overwhelming desire to sleep, but something nagged him. He opened his eyes and looked upwards and saw above him three Indian faces looking down at them both.

He jolted upright and grabbed for his gun and then remembered he'd thrown down his weapons as he'd run after Charlie.

He detected a movement in the body he held. He grasped her closer, glad that the kid had survived.

The Sioux braves did not appear menacing.

'What d'you want?' he asked in a moderately good Sioux dialect.

'We watched you. We saw how you risked your life for the squaw.' The brave bent over and turned Charlie's face so that he could examine it. 'She needs help badly. Come with us and our medicine man will treat her.'

'You mean her no harm?'

The Indian looked at him and laughed.

'We are not demons. We admire bravery and what you did was maybe more than some of our young braves would do. We also don't harm squaws unless they deserve it. This one seems harmless enough.'

McCall struggled to his feet, his muscles stiff and peculiarly weak.

'My horse and my weapons . . . '

'We shall find them, and bring them to you. We believe you are an enemy of the soldiers. We saw you knock down their chief. It was a good punch. You must be a good fighter!'

'You saw all that?'

'Yes, and we saw how the white soldiers reacted to the girl. We do not understand such behaviour.'

McCall grunted and swinging Charlie up in his arms, watched her eyelids flutter.

'She's coming round. Where do we take her?'

The leader showed the way and the other two younger men walked behind.

McCall had mixed feelings as he carried Charlie. She was a small soft bundle, cold and shivery and she clung to him as if she would never let him go.

'Oh, Buff,' she whispered, 'I'm cold and what's happening?'

He held her closer. 'Shush now, don't panic. We're going to the Sioux camp where you'll get help and we hope, something to wear.' He was aware of her body against him. It was strange that now he knew Charlie was a girl, he didn't think of her as a runt to be despised and protected.

He carried her to the Indians' makeshift camp. He looked around swiftly as he lay her down beside a small stone-surrounded fire. This was a small hunting party, out to harass the soldiers but not primarily to kill. Red Cloud must have cautioned the dog soldiers to not go beyond harassment for the time being. He as well as the men in Washington wouldn't want to spark off a wholesale war if talk and agreements could be made.

But the Sioux and the Cheyenne and the other tribes who venerated the Black Hills would only wait so long. If the trickle of miners who were lucky enough to survive the journey and begin their digging for gold became a flood rather than a trickle, then war would follow.

Broken Nose came and squatted by Charlie and looked at her.

'She's young. Why is she expecting to dig for gold? Do all white women take the part of men?'

McCall shook his head.

'She's an exception. Who can tell the ways of the white eyes?'

Broken Nose nodded gravely, his eyes on Charlie's body. She lay hunched up, hands across her breasts and her torn trousers showing part of one buttock. He looked at McCall.

'What will you do with her?' McCall shrugged his shoulders. 'She is your woman, yes?'

McCall remained inscrutable. Inwardly he was startled. Hell! He'd never thought of what should happen to Charlie, now that he was a girl, and as for being his woman, he didn't want to be saddled with a helpless female. Not that she was helpless. She was surprisingly tough, now he thought about it. It took some nerve to appear and act like a boy amongst a band of rough men.

'Yes,' he said slowly, 'she's mine.'

'Good. My young braves' blood runs hot. I shouldn't like them to be sniffing after the squaw instead of keeping their objective in mind.'

'And that is?'

'To keep that camp from being built. To worry at the soldiers' heels until they lose heart and go back to Fort Laramie.'

'And if they fight back?'

'Then they have no time to build or chop down trees or haul their loads back to camp.'

'Why not gather a larger hunting party and massacre them?'

'Because Chief Red Cloud advises caution. A massacre would be the spark for an uprising. The Sioux have lived through terrible punishments inflicted by the military. We do not want to see our best and strongest braves killed unnecessarily.'

'You know of Colonel Carrington?'

'Yes, I know of him. He was one of those present during the powwow at Fort Laramie during the agreement signed to allow the Black Hills to belong for all time to the Indian Nation.'

'And now he is in charge of the men who build the camp in readiness for those who follow with the intention of building forts all along the Bozeman Trail through Wyoming right to the Black Hills themselves. All for the express purpose of protecting those who will violate the Black Hills for the gold.'

Broken Nose scowled.

'He is a man who speaks with a forked tongue. He says one thing and does another.'

'And he is an Indian-hater.'

'But you worked for him as a scout!'

'Yes, but not now. I am free to go my own way.'

'And that is?'

'To ride at your side.'

McCall was aware that someone had silently come up behind him and laid down his weapons and also his discarded smelly shirt, trousers and black army-issue hat.

He looked at them with surprise. Broken Nose smiled.

'Oh, yes, we watched you from the moment you felled the colonel and stripped yourself of your clothes. We see everything. All is known to us. Now I don't think your woman needs our medicine man's help. All she needs is a dry shirt and pants and so I shall leave you to look after her.'

He stalked away and then, turning, looked at McCall. 'From now on, we call you Warbuck. It is more fitting!'

5

'Why the hell play games with me? You could have trusted me!'

McCall watched the girl struggle into his clothes moodily. The time was past for false modesty. He surveyed her slim back as she pulled on the shirt. He still thought of her as a boy. Charlie a girl? It was ridiculous. As for being his woman . . . hell, he'd seen better figures on totem poles! He liked a woman with a bit of shape, something to get hold of, not some skinny half-starved runt!

He wondered whether Broken Nose's reference to her being his woman was some kind of insult. Maybe better not to ponder too deeply, for Broken Nose would have many friends and he was, after all, just a newcomer and a suspect one at that.

He knew he had to live up to his new

name to become truly a blood-brother.

That was one of the things that was making him moody. Did he want to become a Sioux warrior? He had the uncomfortable feeling he didn't belong anywhere.

He looked at Charlie again.

'Well? Why don't you say something?'

Charlie put her hands on her hips. Her eyes glistened with tears of temper and something else.

'I didn't know I could trust you! Pa said I should consider myself a boy and I think he forgot I was ever a girl! He said it was for the best since the West's full of bad men and worse! It was a way of protecting myself. After all, what were you? Just a half-breed scout who might be just as savage as the Sioux stalking the wagon train!'

There was something in her tone that flicked like a whip. It angered him.

'You think because I'm a 'breed I'm something less than an Indian? Neither white nor red. Got the worst traits of both, you think?'

'No, I didn't say that!'

'Your tone said it! Let me tell you, miss, that a man is judged by how he lives, not because of an accident of birth! As a matter of fact, I wouldn't touch your body with a tent pole! I like my women to be real women! Not some petty-minded bag of bones without the makings of womanhood! You're pathetic!'

Now it was her turn to flinch. 'You don't judge a parcel by its wrappings! You look at what's inside!'

'That goes for you too! Do you want me to look at what's in the parcel?'

She blushed. 'I do not! I was speaking generally.'

'Thank you. Now we both know how we stand with each other.'

For a time she sat, pulling on a pair of mocassins, then she shoved her hair back and into his discarded wide-brimmed hat. She looked like a boy again but it was different now. He knew what the parcel contained.

He was ruminating on his position

with the Sioux. Did he want to go or stay? She interrupted his thoughts.

'Buff . . . ' He blinked and looked at her. 'I'm sorry. I do trust you, you know. It was only at first when I just saw the outward you. You were big and smelly and with your beard you were frightening.'

'Me smelly?' McCall looked at her in astonishment. 'Since when have I smelled?'

'All the time. You still do!'

'I damn well don't! I swam in the river before I daubed that mud on myself! I'm fresh as a young fawn!'

'They smell too, and these clothes I'm wearing stink!'

'Well, you're supposed to be a woman, wash 'em!'

'I can't. I've nothing else to wear.'

McCall sighed. 'I'll see what I can do. Maybe there'll be a moonie-squaw amongst this lot. He'll probably bring a spare blanket with him, even on a hunting trip. They like their little luxuries away from home.'

'A moonie-squaw? Never heard of one.'

McCall shrugged. 'They like the boys and they are regarded as gifted soothsayers. If they're good, they accumulate great power and many horses! If you're lucky, you can borrow a blanket until you wash my stink off your clothes!'

She saw he was hurt. 'I'm sorry. I only spoke the truth . . . about you being smelly, I mean. I suppose it was because I wasn't brought up on buffalo fat, just the steaks.'

McCall grunted. 'If you live through a real bad winter out here, you might be glad of rubbing yourself all over with buffalo fat to protect you from the cold!'

'Is that what the Indians do?'

'Yeh, and lots of other things too, like wearing half-cured skins and eating dried jerky and glad of it!'

She pulled a face. Then she said seriously, 'What's going to happen to me, Buff?'

He stared at her. 'That's the big question I've been asking myself. What *will* happen to you?'

'You wouldn't leave me with the Sioux?' She sounded and looked frightened. 'I'd kill myself if you left me!'

She reminded him of a young fawn, big-eyed and twitching, looking all ways and sensing danger and ready to run. Dammit! He was more than a little protective of her. Reluctant but protective and he was conscious of being downed and hog-tied and helpless.

'Look! Stop being dramatic and get the idea of killing yourself out of your mind! Not that you're frightening me none. You'll not hang that over my head. If you do it, it's your business! In fact I'd be free. What ever I decided to do, you wouldn't be holding me back!'

'You wouldn't care?'

'Of course I'd care, but I'm not your keeper. I'd just think I'd failed

97

you somehow and then get on with my life.'

'Maybe I should do it now and get out of your life and you wouldn't have to find me a blanket!'

He slapped her on both cheeks. Two red welts came up in sharp contrast to her white face.

'You hit me!' She put her hands up and covered her face.

'And I'll do it again if you keep snivelling about killing yourself. You're supposed to be a woman, a settler carving out a new life in the west. Where's your courage, Charlie? Lost it when Charlie the boy turned into Charlie, the young girl? By the way, what *is* your name?'

'Charlotte.' She hung her head, unable to look at him.

'Hmm, that figures.' He looked at her broodingly. 'Oh, Charlie, what am I going to do with you?'

Suddenly she was crying as if her heart would break and she flung herself into his arms. He stroked her head, cursing inwardly at this act of fate that made him responsible for her.

'I'm frightened, Buff. You're the only friend I've got!'

He gritted his teeth and looked down at her.

'Don't fret none, kid. I'll see you right. Sometime, somewhere, there'll be a wagon train with white folk on it and they'll look after you and watch out for you. I promise that, kid.'

She looked up at him, eyes clouded and tear-washed. He couldn't fathom what she was thinking, but she didn't seem too impressed. A queer kid was Charlie. He couldn't make her out.

'Well, I'll go find a blanket for you, and you can get my stinking clothes washed and get the smell out of your nose!' His tone was awkward, voice gruff.

A grinning brave produced a horse blanket and offered to do Charlie's washing, which she refused with a hauteur that was an insult to the brave who sulked and walked away muttering about 'goddamn white squaws who needed horsewhipping'.

McCall walked purposefully to the campfire, sank down cross-legged and stared through the flames at Broken Nose sitting opposite. He knew the chief was waiting for him. Waiting to find out his intentions.

'So, you stripped away the trappings of the white army chief. Why?'

'Because I saw the light!'

'Oh? What light?'

'The light of true knowledge.'

'And that is?'

'That I can no longer take orders from the white chief.'

'Is it because of personal differences or for what he stands for?'

'Both. The chief called Colonel Carrington has a black heart. He is not a chief who generates loyalty in his men. I am also sick at heart at what the men in Washington decree about the Black Hills. Those men break promises. Treaties are agreed and torn asunder because of greed. I am ashamed to have white blood in me.'

Broken Nose nodded.

'You speak well for a son whose mother was a Cheyenne, who are our allies in this new struggle. But do you tell the truth, or are you a spy?'

McCall grabbed for his knife and his eyes flashed. Broken Nose sat still, not moving his eyes. He watched McCall steadily.

'If you kill me, I know you as a spy!'

McCall let his knife fall to the ground beside him.

'I'm no spy. I can tell you much about the detail and the orders they ride under but I shall not. There is no need.'

Broken Nose inclined his head.

'That is true. We have no need for disclosures. At this time we are not on the warpath. Chief Red Cloud stays our hands. He is massing the tribes for an attack if the men in Washington do not accede to our demands.'

'So, the orders are to harass and

prevent the permanent camp from being built?'

'That is so.'

'And what are you doing about it?'

'We wait and watch.'

McCall hunched closer, the pine-scented grey smoke from the campfire wreathing him mystically. Broken Nose moved uneasily as he listened to McCall's words.

'I know the white chief's habits. This is what should be done.' Broken Nose's eyes widened as McCall outlined a plan of action.

'But Red Cloud said nothing about abduction! His orders were clear, to watch and wait . . .'

'And give the impression of the Sioux being divided? That they hesitate and wait and bow down to the white men's words? Are the Sioux men to be ordered, when to fight for their rights in the matter of the sacred hills is of the utmost importance? The Cheyenne will not wait for ever!'

Broken Nose's face twisted. He was

angry. He knew, as did all the other subchiefs, that they couldn't hold back their braves for ever.

'The Cheyenne and the other tribes will be ready when Red Cloud gives the word. It will be all-out war. But Red Cloud does not want a confrontation. It would be a loss of lives too great in these times. The tribes' strength is in their young men. Each year there is much loss of life since the white men came.'

'There is no fire in their hearts! If Red Cloud hesitates too long, they will have lost the final battle.' McCall stared through the smoke and flames and Broken Nose had the uneasy feeling he was seeing visions of the future, He was disturbed.

'You speak as if you have inner knowledge. You think kidnapping the white chief could turn the tide?'

McCall shook himself and blinked, breathing in the scent of pine. He felt strange. As if he'd been whisked away and shown a land of peace and plenty.

It was as if he'd glimpsed momentarily a hint of his future.

He saw Broken Nose watching him closely.

'I see it as a necessity. You say Red Cloud's orders were to watch and harass. What more could he want than that the white chief in charge is kidnapped and held to ransom for the saving of the Black Hills.

Broken Nose nodded. He rose smoothly to his feet. 'I shall meditate on this and call a pow-wow of medicine men. In the meantime we watch and wait.'

He stalked away, straight-backed and proud. McCall knew that runners would be sent out and in the depths of the forest a very private pow-wow would take place. He was sure of the outcome. Meanwhile, he must get himself elected to go with the hunting party and watch the troopers and the miners going about their business of hauling timber and building their camp.

They were twenty strong, young

seasoned warriors commanded by Broken Nose's brother, Fox Catcher, a scarred experienced dog soldier in his early forties. Underlying the seriousness, was a spirit of adventure amongst the youths. All needed to count coup to enhance their status in their community. Each warrier carried his coup stick. This harassment business would be a great way to count coup. Not to kill, but touch and harass and to have a witness to prove he'd completed the coup.

They dreamed of going back to their village and recounting their exploits to the village elders and to the womenfolk, and therefore gaining prestige and respect. All their lives they needed to count coup to become worthy of being considered a respected elder in old age.

McCall rode with them. It was a silent approach to the temporary logging camp deep in the forest. McCall noted that the wagons to be used to transport the trimmed tree trunks were drawn into a ring. So the army boys were ready for action and expected a raid.

It was what he would have recommended himself.

He wondered about Fish Eye. Would he be with them?

They tethered the ponies at a distance and a youth, inexperienced in warfare, remained behind to watch them. The others spread out and ringed the camp, watching the stripped-off miners and troopers cut a swathe through the forest to where they were cutting down straight slim pines destined for rough planks to build the palisade before the inner buildings were erected.

McCall saw that already the palisade was taking shape. He saw also that every so many yards a soldier stood on guard. Colonel Carrington was not taking chances.

Captain Platte was in charge, with Corporal Fairbrother dancing attendance on the captain and not looking too pleased about it.

He counted at least twenty men working on the palisade and embankment surrounding it. Half the miners were digging and the rest, he presumed, would be out there cutting trees.

He followed the tracks of the wagons and soon came to the newly cleared area. It was a desolate sight to see. There were piled up branches that already gave off the rank smell of rotting foliage. Piled up trunks lay ready to be hoisted on to wagons and the sound of saws and axes reverberated through the trees. There was no sign of birdlife and no scufflings of small creatures.

McCall watched, bitterly aware that wherever the white man went death and destruction followed. The calm quiet freedom of the forest was shattered; the smell of disquiet lingered in his nostrils.

He recognized several of the troopers working with the miners in their clumsy bid to clear the timber. Here and there was an expert logger who took charge and led his team. One wagon was already loaded, ready to travel back to camp.

He frowned as he saw another wagon still shrouded in canvas. He didn't remember any plans to set up another camp. Perhaps the colonel was underestimating the threat from the Sioux.

He moved silently around, watching and estimating the progress. He was on the lookout for guards. He saw several close by and reckoned that around the area they were working in, there must be at least twenty soldiers on the alert.

So Colonel Carrington was spreading his men thinly, ready for attack from all sides. Then he was jolted by seeing four troopers who he knew worked as a team. What in hell were they doing out in the forest? They should be at the camp ready to defend it with the Gatling gun!

Then it all fell into place. The canvas-covered wagon! By God, it was the reinforced wagon that carried the gun and it was placed strategically to repel a wave of invaders. It could fan from side to side and send a stream of bullets that would cut a swathe through an invading horde before they knew what had hit them!

The first attack would be the last! He must not let it happen!

He crouched low and, keeping to the thick brush, ran silently around the clearing towards the wagon. He must either find Fox Catcher to warn him, or immobilize the Gatling gun himself.

Suddenly a figure rose up before him out of the brush. He raised his hand, his knife at the ready for an attack, then he lowered it as he saw Fish Eye before him with finger to his lips.

'What is it?' Immediately he saw that Fish Eye too, had done away with the scout's military trappings, save for the army-issue rifle. Gone was the hat with the crossed swords; Fish Eye stood straight and tall with head shaved and only a scalplock was left like a coxcomb. This was decorated with three eagles' feathers.

'You too?'

Fish eye nodded. 'This man not stomach what white men do. My ancestors lie in sacred burial ground of my people. I come to warn you about big fire spirit gun. It is primed and ready. All this — ' he waved his hands towards all the buzzing activity of trees being felled, ' — is but a trap. The white chief figures that the Sioux will strike even though it is known that Red Cloud waits for word to come from Fort Laramie from the men in Washington. He reckons Broken Nose is rash and will not wait. He wants him to act now. The gun will speak and Broken Nose's war will be over. There will be much grieving in the tepees and the white chief thinks the Sioux will become sick and move away from Dakota and the Black Hills.'

'If he thinks that he doesn't understand the Sioux!'

Fish Eye stood taller and prouder. He inclined his head.

'We are in the right. We will never bow down to the white man's law, that gives with one hand and takes away with the other! Are you on a scouting party?'

'You could say that. We are to harass, delay and play tricks but not give the soldiers cause to fight. Red Cloud's orders!'

Fish Eye spat into the undergrowth. 'Red Cloud! He's an old woman! We need a new leader! Someone like yourself who knows the mind of this white chief!'

McCall shrugged. 'Broken Nose is a good chief and Fox Catcher an experienced leader.'

'But neither of them has the mind of a seer! Fox Catcher also is known for his temper and not his guile!'

'How come you know so much about them?'

'I am Sioux. I have many friends out there, who think I am one smart Indian to get close to white man's thinking!'

'So what do we do now?'

But Fish Eye never answered that question. There was no need to for suddenly an unearthly scream rent the air and a sporadic burst of gunfire came with shocking suddenness. Then it was as if all the world was on fire. Fox Catcher had disobeyed his orders with a vengeance!

McCall and Fish Eye plunged into the thickets and together surveyed the carnage which was erupting before their eyes. McCall was vaguely aware of Fish Eye firing his rifle into a group of loggers who were scrambling for cover. He saw burning branches being tossed into the shrubbery and the ominous crackle of fire and the smell of burning greenery became stronger.

He saw the danger. The loggers could be burned alive if the wind grew stronger. But more than that, he saw that the wagon carrying the big gun also held the ammunition. If the wagon burned, then it would all go up like an exploding bomb.

He'd seen the devastation caused by

an exploding arsenal, and the troops struggling to clear the tarpaulin from the wagon did not realize their danger.

He'd eaten and joked with those men. They'd drunk together on occasion and been good buddies. What was the matter with him? He was neither white nor red. His loyalties lay in both directions.

Fish Eye had disappeared into the undergrowth and was no doubt trying to reach Fox Catcher. He hoped Fish Eye would blow the reckless fool's brains out.

He had to get to that gun!

A miner with muscles like corded ropes lunged at him, grinning wildly as he swung an axe at him. It would have split his skull in two if it had landed, but McCall kicked him in the gut and, as he jackknifed, plunged his dagger into the man's ribs. He left him gurgling and coughing and loped ahead, intent on reaching the wagon and the gun.

But the gun was now spitting its

lethal charge. It coughed and chattered and the triumphant screams of the Indians were turned to shrieks of horror. A sickly sweet musky smell permeated the air. It brought back memories of other skirmishes during the war and McCall was nauseated.

He had to make his mind up fast. Take out the drinking buddy who was furiously cranking the handle of the gun, or allow him to live and kill Fox Catcher's best braves.

There was no choice. He coolly halted and took aim. His finger faltered on the trigger for a moment as he watched the man's grim face, which he remembered for his friendly grin when they'd drunk together and how he sang sad songs about the girl he left behind him. His trigger finger tightened, and he watched his drinking buddy's face explode into a mass of red pulp.

Sickened, he turned away, giddy and shaken. He'd shot many men in the past but not men he'd fought alongside and lived with. He wanted to run anywhere, to hide his shame, to bury himself . . .

But there was no turning back. Fox Catcher was coming at him, holding a bloody arm.

'It's a trap! Get back! We must muster the men, ready for another attack!'

'If you hold back now, you might as well plunge a dagger into your own heart! We've got to stop that gun!'

Fox Catcher stared at him. 'Warbuck, are you crazy? The fire's closing in and the fire-spirit gun still roars!'

McCall gave a mad laugh. The pain inside him was churning him up. He would be crazy if he didn't try to justify what he'd done.

'Come on, follow me! Rally your dog soldiers, Fox Catcher, if you dare. This is the time to appease the Great Spirit or die trying!'

Fox Catcher gave him a long look, and then raised his head. The Sioux call to rally around the chief echoed through the forest and to the very hills.

Then, from all sides, the Sioux made a mighty effort and during the mêlée that followed, McCall fought his way to the wagon. The scrubland was burning fiercely with a choking dry heat that seared the throat.

There were screams of terror from the beleaguered white men as they fought desperately to keep the fierce fighting Sioux at bay. The hand-to-hand fighting grew more bloody. Leaping Sioux were mown down by the great gun as others followed. Miners and troopers crouched behind wagon barricades until the barricades caught fire, making them withdraw into a tight circle, hampered by screaming horses.

Men died under horses' hooves as well as by arrow and bullet and for McCall the world turned red, a stinking, choking, screaming mass. He felt nothing and everything. There was no fear or emotion as he flung away his rifle and tore and feinted with his knife at every new enemy who challenged him. He felt none of the cuts he sustained, his mind focused on reaching the gun that spat death.

He came to it from the rear, conscious that those who fed and fired the gun had been his friends. The call of his white blood was strong. Instinct urged him to defend them and he fought that insidious weakness as he launched himself at the trooper cranking the huge clumsy machinegun with its six barrels.

The trooper, known as Mad Billy Walsh, was intent on cutting a swathe through the oncoming Indians who'd taken on new life since Fox Catcher's call to attack. Beside Billy was a young trooper, called Acehigh Jack, feeding the ammunition. He was bleeding from a wound in the head and one arm was useless. At their feet lay two crumpled bodies and Mad Billy was working desperately, yelling obscenities at the mob.

McCall sliced into Acehigh Jack, who was too dazed to help himself. McCall saw the look of astonishment on his face as he died under McCall's knife. McCall felt the pain of that. They had spent many hours playing poker together. The feeling was fleeting, for Mad Billy turned. The Gatling gun stopped abruptly as he growled and flung himself at McCall.

'You turncoat bastard,' he bawled. 'I'll rip your guts out!' and the burly trooper went for McCall's wrist, holding off the weapon. It was a silent, grim struggle as Mad Billy panted, a fixed grin on his sweating face, knowing that death for one or both would be the outcome.

McCall flexed his muscles and drew on every ounce of energy. He needed it, for Mad Billy, along with his expertise with the Gatling gun, was a wrestler and had taken on better men than McCall. Mad Billy had never been a friend but he had been a comrade over many years. Now all McCall's inner anger at himself was turned on Billy and he fought with the ferocity of an animal.

They catapulted from the wagon, locked in an unholy embrace. They were unaware of their surroundings as they strained and stretched for supremacy. Yet, however McCall feinted, that hard horny fist was clamped tight over his right hand. He kicked and twisted, kneed Mad Billy in the crotch causing howls of pain, but Mad Billy held on like a leech, gradually turning the wrist so that the knife's point was inches from McCall's heart.

He could feel his heart pounding, strength draining from him. Mad Billy took on giant proportions, a weight impossible to shift.

Then McCall detected a dry slither, a movement in the grass, and instinct warned him of danger from another source. Reaching out with his left hand, he felt the cold coils of a snake. Knowing he had nothing to lose, he grasped it and flung it in Mad Billy's face.

Mad Billy recoiled with shock as the diamond-back hissed and lashed out.

He screamed and let go of McCall's wrist. McCall rolled free, his right hand numb. He grabbed the knife in his left hand and brought it down hard, once, twice and for the third time until Mad Billy's chest gushed blood like a sieve.

Then he staggered drunkenly away into the undergrowth, head hanging low, sick at heart and with no sense of victory. He vomited and it was as if all the bitterness that was in him was purged and he was hollow, his spirit gone from his body.

The next thing he knew, someone was shaking him and hauling him to his feet. Fox Catcher was staring him in the face.

'Warbuck! Can you hear me?' Fox Catcher's face seemed to swim in a fuzzy pool. McCall found it hard to focus.

'Warbuck! Bring back your spirit! The fighting is over!' McCall blinked and gradually his surroundings became sharp and clear. He passed a hand over his forehead.

120

'What happened?'

'The fire-spirit gun . . . you silenced it. It was an awesome sight and the battle between you and the gun handler will be recounted for many moons to come! There will be songs sung about you! Warbuck the mighty! The warrior who fights for the sacred Hills!'

McCall shook his head. 'I just did what had to be done, Fox Catcher. Maybe we won this battle, but there will be others . . . ' His eyes took on a glazed look as of a seer. 'There will be many deaths and much heartache, and in the end, greed will prevail!'

Fox Catcher looked at him strangely. 'You think all this is for nothing?' He waved an arm around the clearing, at the burned wagons, the bodies of the dead lying where they had fallen; already came the sounds of buzzing flies feeding on dead flesh and the whisper of wings in the air as buzzards flew lazily waiting for their feast.

At a distance there was the faint throb of drums beating out their message, but the stillness around was chilling.

'What happened to the troopers?'

'Only a handful left. They took what horses were still standing and took off. We watched them go and did not try to stop them.'

'Good. It must be made plain that the Sioux only attack to protect what is rightfully theirs. I think you understand that, Fox Catcher? To do otherwise would make it hard for Chief Red Cloud to negotiate for a continued peace in Washington.'

Fox Catcher nodded. 'You have much guile, Warbuck. You should be on the war council.'

McCall smiled wearily. 'I am but as an ex-scout, a turncoat in the eyes of the military. I have no training for the politics for peace.'

'Nevertheless I shall recommend you to my brother, Broken Nose, to be elected to the war council.'

'As you wish. But for now I want to walk amongst the dead. There were those whom I respected. One cannot turn a friend into an enemy overnight!'

Fox Catcher watched McCall walk away, a slight frown between his eyes. He didn't understand McCall. Either a man was a friend or an enemy. McCall worried him. But then, he was halfbreed, a product of two cultures, a man looked down on by the red men. If he had been fighting shoulder to shoulder with the army, Fox Catcher would have killed him without compunction.

Maybe he shouldn't recommend McCall for the war council after all.

He went away to supervise the retrieval of the dead dog soldiers, but to be on the safe side he would forbid the taking of scalps . . . for this occasion.

McCall walked amongst the dead troopers. He knew he was looking for one special person. He soon found him surrounded by a number of dog soldiers. He'd sold his life dearly. His empty hand-gun was by his side, a bloodied knife near his hand and his body and arms were slashed and now infested with buzzing flies. Captain James Platte, who'd made life under Colonel Carrington bearable. He'd never once referred to McCall's parentage and always treated him with respect.

There had been times when Platte had saved his life on patrol, and he had done likewise. There had been a subtle bonding between them. Platte had trusted his ability to scout and bring back accurate information, and on rare occasions he'd torn down the public mask and shown himself as a man who could worry about his men and his family back home.

Now McCall chased off the flies which rose in an angry mass and moved on. He wiped the calm face and closed the staring eyes, and then, on impulse, scooped up the body. He would return Platte to the temporary camp for Colonel Carrington to give a full military burial, that was, if the colonel hadn't decided to withdraw and admit defeat and go back to Fort Laramie. In that event, McCall would take the body back to Fort Laramie.

Fox Catcher eyed him with alarm. 'What do you intend to do, Warbuck?'

McCall stared at him coldly. 'He was my friend. I take him back to the camp for burial.'

Fox Catcher was nonplussed. 'A burial party will come back for all the soldiers.'

McCall shrugged. 'And in the meantime, they are all prey to the animals? This will not happen to the captain. I take him back.'

Fox Catcher nodded. 'I will find you horses.'

The body, head down, feet dangling, was hoisted on to a nervous animal who smelled death and didn't like his burden. Fox Catcher watched him ride away before going back to the task of robbing the dead troopers of anything valuable, including rifles and ammunition. The Gatling gun was a twisted wreck, having fallen from the burning wagon which held it. It was of no use to the Indians and would never be used again by the soldiers.

McCall made his slow way back to the temporary camp. While he did so he sent up a prayer for Captain Platte's safe journey into a new life.

The temporary camp was in chaos. There was a lack of wagons, too few men to defend it and Colonel Carrington was in panic. He had lost his able officers; the miners and labourers were in revolt and his only hope was that a messenger he'd sent posthaste to Fort Laramie would send reinforcements and new instructions.

He was crouched low over a map on a table in an open-sided tent when the rider came galloping into camp, followed by a horse carrying a body. The rider pulled up outside the tent in a flurry of dust.

'Colonel Carrington, sir! I've brought you Captain Platte. It was the least I could do for him! Bury him deep, Colonel, guard him well!' McCall dropped the reins and whirling around, dug his heels into his own horse and galloped out of camp before Colonel Carrington could gather his wits or grab for his revolver.

'I'll get you, McCall!' he bawled, shaking his fist. 'You halfbreed no-good son of a bitch! You renegade bastard!'

Then as one of the troopers grabbed for the loose reins and calmed the frightened horse, he wondered why McCall had risked bringing the captain in.

He approached horse and man. Lifting the captain by the hair he saw that his eyes were closed and that there was no sign of mutilation. The cuts were evidence of his fighting for life. Carrington scratched his chin.

Why had McCall returned him? Was there a semblance of loyalty in the man despite his defection? Did a white man's blood count after all?

He glanced at the waiting trooper. 'Right, Scheifer, take him away and rustle up a burial party. When you're ready, call me, and I'll say a few words.'

Then he went back to his map and worked on a route which would snake its way for hundreds of miles to the Black Hills.

But his mind wasn't on routes. Would he ever live to see that trail being used by adventurers and government officials intent on digging out fortunes for themselves?

He flung down ruler and pen and dug out a bottle of whiskey. He drank it neat from the bottle.

'Oh, to hell with everything!' he muttered and took another swig.

6

McCall laughed as he rode away, through the camp and beyond. He noted as he went that not much progress had been made. It would be easy to attack and annihilate before the outer defences were part-way finished. He remembered Colonel Carrington's shock and surprise and the twisted hate on his face. The good colonel had never liked him. He was one of those white men who made the reputations for the rest . . . an Indian hater, who loudly declared to all who would listen that a good Indian was a dead Indian.

While such men lived, then the Indian nations and the white invaders could never know a real peace.

McCall realized that the only way to deal with the colonel was to make him admit defeat and go back to Fort Laramie and confess his failure. He would take much joy in that.

As he rode back to the Sioux camp, he pondered on it. It might be a good policy to leave the military camp alone for a while. Fox Catcher wasn't a wily leader. His idea was to go in, attack and withdraw and harass the enemy. He would lose valuable braves that way.

It would be best to let the colonel keep busy, watch and wait and then, when the time was right, before the defences were complete, attack, fire the buildings and burn everything to the ground. There would be no warning. No quarter.

Fox Catcher listened gravely to McCall's plan. He wasn't sure whether he approved of it. The Sioux were not used to waiting and calculating. He wanted action.

'If we wait, the white chiefs will send more soldiers to take the place of those who were lost!' he protested.

'It will take time. Messages must be sent, decisions taken and arrangements made for troops to be deployed from other areas. It cannot be done overnight. We shall watch for them coming and two days from the camp we shall strike. The cavalry will come too late! They too will be helpless to defend themselves if they have no fortress camp to occupy.'

Fox Catcher nodded slowly. 'Have we enough men? Or should I send to Broken Nose for more help? He has many villages to call on.'

'Perhaps if you send a messenger and ask his advice on the matter?'

'Hmm, he will expect me to make my own decisions.'

'So, make your decision!'

'If our band grows bigger, then what shall we do? I cannot keep the Sioux warriors in idleness. They will want action or they will go back to their villages.'

McCall wondered how Fox Catcher ever got his name. There was nothing about the sly fox about him. He concluded he was a sub-chief only because he was Broken Nose's brother. He sighed. It wasn't lost on Fox Catcher.

'I have never been in this situation before,' Fox Catcher confessed, a little shamefaced. 'My usual duties are to arrange buffalo hunts, skirmish with neighbouring villages over water rights and hunting grounds, not take on the white soldiers.'

, 'I see. Then what about keeping your braves busy watching the trails going to the Black Hills? The rumour of gold will bring many white men prepared to dig into the Hills. They too have to be harassed and turned back. Some will die and they will be a warning to others who will come.'

'You think there will be many?'

'The white men are like locusts. They are uncountable and will be unstoppable if they once get a foothold in those hills. They are even now there, digging their mines and torturing the land. I know it. The colonel has despatches sent from Washington.

Already the rape of the Hills has started!'

'Then we must do what we can to stop the wagon trains. I will send for more braves and we shall use your plan.'

'Good.' McCall smiled. He hoped he would come face to face with the hated colonel when the permanent camp was burned to the ground. Those forts planned to be built from Fort Laramie and Piney Ridge to the Black Hills would never take place.

Red Cloud would be pleased. It would give him time to negotiate a new settlement. Those men in Washington would realize the threat of all-out war. They would be fools if they didn't understand the danger.

But the word gold did strange things to white men's minds. McCall had a strange cold feeling running up and down his spine. Would all the protesting and harassment be in vain? Suddenly he was sickened. He longed to be free, to hunt and live with nature. To feel the breeze on his face and smell the virgin forest and know the inner peace of living as nature intended.

But he was committed to the Comanche and the Sioux. It was his dead mother's right that he should be.

He went to look for Charlie. He . . . she . . . was a problem. He must get her back to her own people.

She watched him come to her, the smooth rolling gait that denoted litheness and control of all his muscles always stirred her. He reminded her of a cautious wild animal putting each foot down delicately as if it could feel any living thing moving under its foot. She reminded herself that that was what he was, a man used to the wilds, experienced in silent passage, his life depending on that smooth easy movement.

He looked at her, crouched near the small fire that did not give off much tell-tale smoke. A warband always lived either without fire or with carefully selected dry fuel so that the colourless smoke drifted high into the sky and was lost.

'You all right? You look pale.'

'I was worried about you. I thought perhaps . . . ' She looked away, biting her lip. She couldn't tell him of the awful dread that had overcome her earlier in the day. That he might die and that she would be forever kept prisoner amongst the Sioux. There was another realization too, which had shocked her. She wanted him alive and she wanted to be with him . . . always.

'You thought I might be killed?'

'Yes.'

'And you worried what might become of you?'

'Yes. Wouldn't you if you were me?' She sounded bitter and frightened and a little hysterical.

'It might not be so bad living with the Sioux. They make good loyal husbands.'

'They smell of rancid fat!'

'You'd get used to it!'

Colour stained her pale cheeks with

temper. She wasn't a bad-looker when she got all fired-up. It was quite a diversion teasing her. His lips quivered in amusement as she sprang at him, fingers spread to claw him.

'You bastard! Is that all you can say, cool as you please, that I would get used to a dirty smelling Sioux?'

'Hey there, just a minute. Don't go making fool remarks about a people you don't know!' He gripped her wrist hard until he felt her tremble and sag and then he loosed her warily, waiting to see if she would attack him again. 'You're lucky Fox Catcher or one of his snoopers wasn't around to hear you.'

She looked sullen and rubbed her wrist. 'You hurt me. I'll have a bruise tomorrow.'

'Better than a sore ass. I should have whipped you!'

'You wouldn't dare!'

'Oh no? Another tantrum like that one and I'll soon show you if I dare or not!'

She gave him a long hard look.

'You're a savage like they are, and to think I worried about you! Made myself sick to my stomach thinking you might be lying somewhere hurt! God! How I hate myself for being so foolish!'

She turned to run from him, tears welling in her eyes. He caught her and whirled her to him so hard she rammed him in the chest. He held her tightly and looked down into her eyes.

'What is all that supposed to mean?'

She looked up at him, noting the hard eyes, the tiny crows' feet and the smooth tanned skin above the black beard. She breathed the smell of him, felt his heart beat rhythmically against hers and the heat from him melted her bones. It was as if she was hypnotized by him.

'I'm not sure. I think I love you!'

For half a dozen heartbeats he held her and then he pushed her away from him as the shock of her words penetrated.

'You're only a kid. You don't know what you're saying! You're crazy! Why, only a few days ago you were a boy and a young 'un at that!' He took a deep breath. 'There's only one thing for it. As soon as I'm able I'll return you to Fort Laramie where there's sure to be some good folk who'll take you in and give you a home. You should be with white folk.'

'No! I don't want that. I want to be with you! I feel safe with you. What is there for me back amongst white folk? I'll be someone's unpaid servant, or a saloon girl if I don't want to be a wife. There's nothing else for me. Don't you understand? You would send me back to hell!'

He looked at her, perplexed. She was such a little thing. Again she reminded him of a young fawn which had lost its mother.

As once before, he said it again. 'Oh, Charlie, what am I going to do with you?'

She dropped to her knees in front of him, hugging his legs. 'Please . . . please, Buff, don't send me away.

You're all the family I've got. I can cook for you and wash your clothes and if you wish it, I'll stay away from you and I'll never ever argue with you. I'll do everything you say! I swear it!'

He pulled her upright. He held her close, his hand caressing her head, her long hair tangling in his fingers.

'Very well. But it won't be easy. Anytime you want to change your mind, you've only got to say. Right?'

'Right!' She smiled up at him and it was like the sun coming out after a rainstorm. She loosened herself from him. 'I'll go and see what I can find for you to eat.' She fairly danced away, humming a little tune to herself.

McCall watched her go. He remembered the old Indian legend his mother used to tell, about the old man who saved a boy's life and so, for evermore, he was responsible for his life. But the boy climbed on his shoulders and became a burden. In time the old man didn't notice the burden. When finally the boy grew tired of being carried and jumped off him and ran away, then the old man mourned the passing of his burden and hated his freedom.

He wondered if he too would hate it if he was free of her.

She brought him food, sat cross-legged and watched him eat. Afterwards she took and washed his dishes at the stream.

He saw how the younger braves watched her and knew that to them she must indeed be his squaw.

That night when they bedded down near the fire he felt her tuck herself into his back for warmth. He smiled into the darkness and felt mighty comfortable. He slept and dreamed that she'd run away and he'd followed her, shouting her name. He woke up in a hot sweat; she was sitting up looking down at him.

'What is it, Buff? Were you fighting again? You were calling out and yelling.'

'Something like that, Charlie. I'm

sorry I disturbed you.' He had to lie. He couldn't tell her the truth. She would think him crazy. 'Let's settle down again to sleep. It'll soon be dawn.'

When he finally awakened, he felt the place cold beside him, only the imprint of her on the blanket. He started up in panic. Had she wandered away?

He rubbed his hand over his forehead and noted its shaking. What in hell was the matter with him?

Then he saw her emerge from the undergrowth. Her hair was wet and he realized she'd been washing in the stream. He looked as if he was angry with her, for the relief was painful.

'Is something the matter?' She looked at him half-fearful.

He shook his head, confused. She worried him. He didn't want her around and yet he was frightened of losing her. It was most strange. 'I'm hungry. I just want to eat.'

'Oh! I'm sorry. I should have thought of that before I went to bathe. I'll get

141

you something now,' and she darted away.

'No! Wait!' But she was out of earshot and making her way to the youth who was already carving strips of meat that had been roasting overnight amongst hot stones.

Goddammit! McCall cursed inwardly. I don't want Charlie to think I only want her as a slave! He rubbed his forehead distractedly and got up, stretching.

It was then that he made his decision. They would have to part, because he knew that he could not exploit her and it wasn't fair on him or her for them to become too close. He knew his limitations. He was a halfbreed, not fitting in anywhere, and a girl like her would want a home and security and the trappings of civilization. That was something he couldn't give her. He needed to be free.

So, they must part, but he would keep his decision to himself until the time was right. Then, no begging and pleading would make any difference; he would find her a good home.

But now there were other problems. He was committed to the Sioux for as long as it took. He had given his word and until the situation about the Black Hills was resolved, he must help in any way he could. He owed it to his mother and all the Cheyenne, to fight for and revere the sacred Hills.

Someday he would go back there, and make his peace with the sacred place his mother had taken him to when he was a child. He would give homage to the sun and the sky and the wind and the rain and running water and all living things.

He sensed his need and growing closeness with nature. It called to him to become a free spirit.

Someday he would answer that call.

Now there were more serious problems. He would eat and seek out Fox Catcher and Broken Nose and plan a new defence of the sacred Hills. They cried out to him for help. Did no one else hear the cry?

And so McCall found himself in a circle surrounding a ritual fire that glowed but did not have flames leaping high. It cast an orange-blue glow because of what had been sprinkled on it by the medicine man known as Wise Owl.

He looked about him at the elders and the subchiefs who, obeying the commands of Broken Nose, now gathered together. He saw not only Oglala Sioux representatives, but members of the lesser tribes who were friendly, the Arapaho and Gros Ventre as well as Cheyenne. He marvelled at the influence of the Black Hills on these differing tribes.

As he watched, he had a vision that someday there would be a great uprising. More tribes would join the crusade against the white man.

A coldness swept through him. It would not be yet. Many moons would pass before the final outcome. There would be many deaths and many sacrifices made.

It came to him then that it was how a man lived and fought and believed in what he was doing that mattered, not the final outcome.

He saw these older experienced chiefs watching him. Already there were mutterings about Warbuck and his strategy. He was looked up to for his experience with military matters, not because of himself as a man.

Broken Nose rose to his feet and circled the ring of chiefs. A distant drumbeat heralded the beginning of the pow-wow. Broken Nose lifted the peace-pipe high into the sky and gave the mournful 'Ayahh . . . ah . . . '

Then, inhaling, he sent a wisp of smoke high into the sky. Then bowing, he handed the pipe to Fox Catcher, who offered it to the Cheyenne Chief, Buffalo Horn in respectful deference as the most senior chief to himself.

Soon, the pipe travelled round and round, and after each inhaling the chief passing on the pipe would make a point and ask a question or give an answer.

Gradually it became clear that McCall's superior knowledge of the military mind won supporters and the plans were made.

He explained military tactics for the benefit of those ignorant of the white man's way of battle.

The outcome was that the camps and forts should be surrounded during the rising of the full moon in the Month of Fat.

Then, simultaneously, they should attack. Always providing that the big chief, Red Cloud, lost his appeal with the big white chiefs in Washington.

Attacking at the same time would mean that no troops could travel to help a beleaguered fort or camp.

A fiery Arapaho chief stood up and waved his arms. 'Why should we wait? Why not attack now? Are we frightened sheep that wait for white men's decisions? They broke their covenant! Must we grovel for their convenience?'

'You are too hasty!' McCall was impelled to shout. 'Would you have Indian blood on your hands if it could be avoided?'

The Arapaho looked at McCall with scorn. 'You are as nothing! Why should we listen to you? You could be leading us into a trap!'

McCall felt a surge of anger. He rose to his feet in one lithe movement and stalked towards the angry chief. 'You take back those words, or you die!'

The Arapaho's answer was to whip out his knife from his belt and drop into a crouch. 'Never! You white man's bastard!'

Around them, the chiefs sat quiet and watched.

McCall whipped out his own knife and, watching the chief's eyes, circled him warily. He knew he must damp down his anger, or leave himself open to any rash movement on the chief's part.

He waited. It was best to watch and

assess and wait for the first assault. It soon came. With a yell, designed to intimidate, the Arapaho leapt forward, arms swinging, knife making a whistling sound as it cut through the air. McCall sprang aside. Parrying the blow he brought his foot up and caught the man in the stomach.

He heard the gasp and the exhaling of breath as the Indian rolled with the blow. Then McCall went after him, his knife swinging wildly, but a last minute jab of a fisted punch rocked him back on his heels.

He just had time to clear his head when the Arapaho came in screeching and whipping wildly with his knife, slashing at McCall's face and shoulder.

He felt the searing touch of the knife and the stickiness of blood as his reflexes jerked him sideways. Then he too was wielding his knife with devastating results. Two direct hits. Blood spouted from shoulder and thigh of the chief. Glaring madly, his hate-filled eyes held McCall's.

'White Eye spawn! You'll not live to lead us to disaster! You're a spy . . . ' His head came down in a savage butt to McCall's chest.

It felt like a battering ram. But the words had given McCall time to gather his wits and energy. He saw the head coming at him in that split second which counted. He reeled backwards and drew up his legs. He kicked out as he catapulted backwards. He was aware of the Arapaho's body lifting into the air.

He lay winded on the ground and heard the gasps of the circle of watching men. Then raising himself on one elbow, he saw the chief spread-eagled across the dampened-down fire.

He saw the body start to quiver as the heat engulfed it. Then he heard the screams. He looked about him. No one moved. Not even the chief's own men came to his assistance.

McCall dragged himself painfully upright and staggered over to the chief lying amidst the embers. He stared down at him.

'Help me!' The eyes stared up at him desperately.

McCall saw the mute appeal and reached down and dragged the man clear. There was the smell of burnt flesh.

McCall put a foot on the stricken man's chest and looked around him.

'All you here are witnesses. I have a right to kill this man. He insulted my parents and myself. I leave him his life, what is left of it. This is not weakness on my part. For him, it is worse to live than to die!' He looked and found where the Arapaho chief's followers were.

'Take him away!' McCall walked wearily back to his place in the circle and sat down.

7

Colonel Carrington faced his superior officer, General Morton. He felt like a naughty schoolboy up before his headmaster, waiting to receive six of the best on his twitching ass.

He listened to the tirade until his ears ached. He'd never known General Morton in such a rage that his very moustache quivered. The man stuttered and spat drops of saliva down his pristine fresh uniform.

'Sir, if you would listen . . . '

'Goddammit. man, I'm sick of listening! What the hell's the matter with you boys these days? In my day, we would have gone out and had us a field day, shooting down those Indians like so much carrion! I say you're not using the right tactics! You're a fool and a blunderer, Carrington, and if you're not careful you'll be back in the ranks stripped down to the bone, by God!'

'Sir, about Piney Ridge . . . '

'I don't want to hear another word about Piney Ridge! The camp was burned to the ground and we're no further forward as to the other forts. There's men in Washington after my guts for this delay, Colonel. What are you going to do about it?'

'Sir, we're short of men. We're spread too thinly everywhere. We need replacements, fresh weapons and ammunition as well as wagons and horses. There is also a need for a new recruitment drive concerning civilian labourers. There is a reluctance to face the Sioux . . . '

'Goddammit! They're no more of a danger than they used to be!'

'Sir, they're using military tactics.'

'Nonsense! It's your poor leadership! You need a tactician, someone to do your thinking for you!'

Carrington's face turned a dull red. He ground his teeth, hating the general and the cursed half-breed who'd brought about this situation. He'd get the bastard if he had to die to do so!

'Sir, with due respect, you have no idea what we're up against. Since those men you speak of in Washington are still debating whether to keep to their covenant with the Five Nations concerning the Black Hills, the Indian tribes have banded together and are ready for all-out war. You do understand that?'

'Of course! They've always been ready for war! I suppose it's part of their upbringing. If they don't make war against us, they make war with each other. It's a way of life.'

'But now they're much more dangerous. They're being led by the halfbreed they call Warbuck.'

General Morton scratched into his white beard. 'Warbuck. I've heard rumours of this upstart. Wasn't he one of your scouts, Colonel?'

'He was, sir.'

'Then why didn't you control him?

How many years did he serve you?'

'Ten, sir.'

'Hmm, then you should have instilled loyalty in him in that time, surely, Colonel? What happened?'

'Sir,' Carrington was reluctant to speak. 'He was a hard man to understand, sir. We never saw eye to eye about things, sir.'

'And why was that? You don't have to understand a man, Colonel to generate loyalty. There are other ways.'

'Sir, as I said, he was a halfbreed.'

'And you have difficulty in accepting that?' There was a new hardness in General Morton's voice.

'What he was coloured my judgement of him. I saw him as a betrayer of his mother's people. Not someone I could put my trust in and I was right. He quit army employ just at a time when he was required to do his job. He turned renegade.'

'There must have been a reason?'

Carrington coughed. 'He was insubordinate. There was a difference of opinion which escalated . . . '

'Goddammit, Colonel! Stop this pussyfooting around! I had a report on my desk that you goaded this man beyond reason for many years until he cracked. Am I right?'

'Sir, I cannot abide halfbreed bastards!'

'Thank you for being frank. It was like pulling teeth!' he said with thinly veiled sarcasm. He drummed his fingers on the desktop. 'So, through your stupidity, the Five Nations got themselves a leader well versed in military tactics and how it shows! Reports are coming in of so many skirmishes that are keeping the divisions holed-up in forts all around the region. There are roving bands in hit-and-run raids, preventing prospectors going into the Hills and making it impossible for troops to move. What are you going to do about it, Colonel?'

'Sir,' Carrington licked his lips. 'As I pointed out, there is a lack of men . . . '

'You either stop this Warbuck or you

finish your career cleaning out latrines! Dismissed!'

Carrington stiffened in shock, saluted smartly and turned, leaving the general to shake his head and drum his fingers once more on his desk before reaching for a sheaf of reports. How in hell was he to retrieve the situation without telling those know-it-all penpushers back in Washington to get their fingers out from up their asses, climb down and give the Indian trash the assurances they were willing to die for. God rot their stinking carcases!

Outside the office Carrington drew a deep breath. He knew his blood pressure was sky high. He could feel the blood drumming in his ears. A curse on the general! And a double curse on Buff McCall who was now Warbuck, the Sioux's new wonderboy.

Two of his aides were waiting for him with his horse. He climbed aboard without a word to his men and with a brusque nod set off back to the barracks. On the way, his mind went over the interview. There must be a way to bring Warbuck out into the open.

When they reached the barracks Carrington strode into his temporary quarters and nodded to Captain Baines, his new captain who replaced the dead Platte.

'I want to talk to you, Captain. Privately.'

'Sir?' Carrington looked at a sergeant who was sitting with Baines. Baines nodded a dismissal and followed the colonel into the tiny cell-like room which was both sleeping-place and office.

'Captain, we're on a ride to nowhere.'

'Sir?'

'We're between a rock and a hard place. The general's given us orders to find and take Warbuck, or else!'

'Or else what, sir?'

'Use your head, Captain. We're all for the slippery slope if we don't succeed.'

The captain went white. Gone would

be any hope of promotion if he and the Colonel couldn't come up with a plan of action. 'What the hell are we to do, Captain?'

Captain Baines coughed, fished for a handkerchief and blew his nose to give him time to think, his wits working overtime.

The Colonel was no good at manoeuvring. He'd found that out within days of joining him on his staff. The colonel rode on the backs of anyone who'd carry him. The only idea he had was a logical one.

'We'll have to promote a stampede to the Hills. That'll bring Warbuck out into the open.'

'You fool! We've got to walk a thin line! We don't want to start an all-out war!'

Then Carrington stroked his chin and considered, staring at the disgruntled Captain Baines. He pursed his lips. Then, smiling, he clapped Baines on the back.

'You know, Captain, maybe you've

got something after all. Perhaps a few rumours here and there, a trickle of prospectors taking risks, hoping for a quick strike and out before the Indians are aware of what's going on, eh, Captain?'

Captain Baines nodded hopefully, aware that the Indians, damn them, would know exactly what was going on. They had their spies camped out permanently. Didn't the stupid colonel realize that? How else would those raids occur just at the right time?

'Sir, we could send out more scouts to mingle with Warbuck's followers and find out his intentions.'

'Hmm, but can we trust them? Warbuck was one of ours.'

'Yes, but not a traditional enemy of the Sioux. Might I point out that we have at least three scouts who would deem it an honour to infiltrate Warbuck's band.'

'Well, what have we to lose if they don't succeed? It's worth a try. You brief them, Captain, and offer the usual incentives for success and loyalty. They prize extra liquor, beads and a modern rifle above cash. See to it, Captain.'

★ ★ ★

McCall was weary. Charlie sat opposite him, overjoyed at seeing him again but anxious because he'd lost weight. They sat alone, a little away from the rest of the band who'd ridden into the Indian village with him.

They were drinking and re-telling their exploits, laughing as they took it in turns to count coup. Around them, listening and enjoying the small victories were the women and the older men of the village and the young boys not yet ready to come to full manhood.

McCall watched them with sadness. He couldn't bring himself to join them. Something in him rebelled at recounting tales of murder against white men.

It was at these times that he knew

he was different from them. He had no tribal loyalties. His war against the white eyes was because of their profanity in allowing the sacred places to be fouled and defiled, not against the white men for themselves.

The Indians he led knew he was different. They used him for their own ends but he doubted if they would mourn and give him the spirit rites if he was killed.

He belonged nowhere.

Now he looked at Charlie. It was time to make the great decision and he braced himself. She had grown on him during the last few months. He missed her when they were apart and relied on her during those times when he rested between skirmishes.

She was shrewd too for a girl. She watched and warned him of jealousies amongst the braves, of gossip gleaned from the women when they worked together, drawing water and grinding corn.

She kept him posted with the

rumours heard. She was the one who alerted him about Colonel Carrington's troops converging on to the flatlands below the Black Hills.

'You think he's waiting for you, Buff?' she'd asked fearfully.

He'd smiled.

'Of course! Wouldn't you if you were he?'

She'd bit her lip. 'Are you not afraid?'

'No. I think the time will come when we must face each other. We both hate and it eats us away. Something must be resolved.'

Now he cleared his throat and watched her. Her fingers were busy working on a leather jerkin for him. She had grown adept at Indian ways. She could find roots and herbs in the forest and knew the places to find quails' eggs and even on occasion find a bees' nest by following the spoor of a bear.

She was self-reliant and brave. He felt the loss that he would know when she was gone.

'Charlie,' his tone of voice made her look up sharply.

'Yes, Buff, what is it?'

'You'll have to leave. Soon, there will be all-out war. The men in Washington are dragging their feet. They do not want to lose face. Red Cloud is getting impatient. Any day now a message will come and there will be a big gathering and there will be danger for all white people.'

'But I'll be safe here, Buff. I know these people.'

McCall shook his head. 'You don't when the blood lust is on them. The women will not save you. It will be the dog soldiers from other tribes who will take you. You must go to where you will be safe!'

'But . . .'

'No buts, Charlie.' He raised a hand to stay her argument. 'There is a strong caravan moving along the Bozeman Trail, not heading for the hills. You will join them. I shall take you myself. It is for the best, Charlie.'

'No! I don't want to go! You can't make me! I'll appeal to Broken Nose! He will persuade you to let me stay. He looks kindly on me!'

'Not enough to go against me, Charlie. He also knows the risks because we have talked of this. Please . . . no bad words between us. Gather what you want to take with you and we leave at dawn.'

She held up his jerkin. 'I haven't finished this. I can't go before I see you wearing it.' Her voice broke. 'Moonflower says it is a bridal garment, made and given by a bride to her husband. Don't you want me, Buff?'

He swallowed. Hell, she was making it hard for him. Goddammit, he wasn't a eunuch. He had his desires, but knowing they must part, he had held himself in check. It wasn't right to send a white girl back to civilization without her maidenhead intact. If she hadn't that she would have no status in white man's society.

As it was, she would have to live with

164

the stigma of consorting with Indians, unless she could travel so far away that no one knew her history.

'Buff . . . please . . . ' Suddenly she was in his arms, her lips seeking his. 'Buff . . . don't you . . . love me just a little?' Her voice broke and he could feel the tension in her.

Against his will he held her close, his mouth on hers. Her lips felt like liquid fire, stirring urges he'd been confident he kept under control.

Her tongue sought his. The contact fused them together and stars and sparks exploded in McCall's head. This was no child clinging to him, she was a woman with all a woman's instincts to attract her man.

For a long moment the kiss lasted, and then he tore her from him. He was gasping with the effort of control. He shoved her away from him abruptly.

He saw the hurt in her face as she covered her lips with the back of her hand.

'Charlie, it would be wrong! Look

at me! I'm a man belonging nowhere! I have no place in a civilized world. I'm too old to change. You're young. You'll make a new life amongst people you understand. You'll find someone else to love!'

She shook her head. 'I'll never meet anyone like you. I don't only love you, Buff, but I trust and respect you. Doesn't that mean something?'

He shook his head. She was making it so hard. He was aware of his hand shaking as he ran his fingers through his hair.

'You're making a mistake, Charlie. I'm no hero. Don't you see? I'm the nearest thing to a white man you've seen since your pa died. You're confused. Why don't you think of me as a father-figure? You'll be glad someday when you meet the right man.'

She stood up and took several steps backwards, away from him. She was shaking.

'You're a fool, Buff McCall! You're

blind and stupid and I hope you live long enough to feel the misery I feel now!' She turned and ran away towards the women's quarters.

He watched her go, a great sadness overwhelming him.

'Believe me, girl, I know that misery already!' he whispered but there were only the night prowlers and the breeze to hear.

He lay awake all night, battling with himself, but he knew it had to be done. Charlie had to have her chance of life with her own kind.

The decision had to be made, for the wagon train he'd chosen for her to join was steadily heading west and would soon be too far ahead to catch up.

The importance of that train was that he knew the wagon master from the days of his youth. Ned Bascombe had spent thirty years carrying freight and leading families west. He could leave Charlie in his care knowing that Ned would see her settled with some kind-hearted family.

He also had some savings in a pouch which he would give Ned to use on her behalf, of which Ned could have one quarter if he delivered her safely to her new home. The rest would be his gift to her. There would be enough for a dowry. Charlie would not be a penniless bride.

He refused to think of her with another man. That possibility was something he would never ponder on. All he wanted was for Charlie to be happy.

It was before dawn when he entered her tepee, clapping a hand over her mouth as she struggled to scream. He didn't want to rouse the village. The Sioux would never understand his motives for taking her away. They would think him strange and unnatural. As it was, they were intrigued that Warbuck did not sleep in the white girl's tepee.

She stared up at him with fear, her eyes wide and imploring but he resisted their plea. Silently he bound her wrists and ankles and carried her quietly to where the horses were corralled. He had hastily packed what he thought she would need in a parfleche, the native leather bag that could carry everything from clothing, artefacts and food, and it was now firmly tied on to a gentle mare. He sliced the thongs tying her feet and flung her like a sack of corn on to the mare's back. Then he untied his own horse and holding her reins firmly leapt aboard, leading her away from the village.

'I should scream,' she said savagely.

'Why didn't you?'

'Because I didn't want either of us to be figures of fun to those people.'

'A good enough excuse. They're my sentiments exactly.'

'So you've had this planned all the time?'

'Yes.'

'You really are going through with it, even when I told you . . . I loved you?'

'Yes.'

169

They rode on for a while as it sank in what it meant to her. Then she turned to him.

'You're a twisted halfbreed bastard, Buff McCall, and I'll never forgive you! And I'll never again look upon you as a friend, never mind the man I loved best in the world! I'd rather die than stay in your company longer than necessary!'

'I'm sorry there's bitterness between us, Charlie. I didn't want it that way. Someday you'll really understand. You've got a life. Mine is nearly over.'

She sat her horse, stiff-backed and looking straight ahead. She wouldn't let him see the gathering tears. She'd rather have an arrow rammed into her back than allow him to see her distress. God damn him to hell!

She didn't look as if she'd heard his words.

They rode on.

Time passed in a blur. She was bone-weary and lost count of the hours they rode, or the short nights spent under the stars. She slept the sleep of exhaustion and never knew that he lay most nights awake, tormenting himself at what he was impelled to do.

Then came the morning when they crossed new tracks and McCall, after studying them, reasoned they'd caught up with Ned Bascombe's wagon train.

His heart lurched. The parting would soon be upon them and then it would be over. A sweet episode in a life that had not known much pleasure.

He quickened their pace. They could be with the wagon train when it camped for the night. He would stay long enough to eat and jaw with Ned Bascombe and explain Charlie's need for a good home; that she wasn't some adventurous young whore but a respectable girl left orphaned, and he would trust Ned to seek out a good family.

He would also listen to the latest gossip, find out what was new about the Black Hills and what steps might have been taken. Any titbit of gossip could be useful.

Then it would be hard riding to get back to the Sioux village and report anything important that might have been gleaned.

He was also anxious to receive news about the raids taking place amongst the sprawling hills, and whether the tide of prospectors was being turned.

Just how effective were those raids? And were they important enough to justify the deaths of so many young braves?

Suddenly he lifted his head and listened. He couldn't be imagining it, could he? He could hear the sporadic firing of rifles. He looked at Charlie and saw that she too was aware of the sound and what it meant.

He bent towards her without a word, and slashed loose the thongs he'd prudently kept about her wrists for fear she had some hare-brained scheme of riding off into the wilderness.

She rubbed her wrists and looked at him.

'It's the wagon train, isn't it, Buff?

It's being attacked.' She couldn't keep a note of glee out of her voice.

He gritted his teeth. The little bitch was happy about the situation!

'I'm going to climb up the escarpment and take a look-see. You can either make a cold camp and dig out some of that dried meat and get some water from that stream over there in the coffeepot, or I'll lash you to a tree. Which is it to be?'

'I'll make camp.'

'Good. Then I'll take a peep and see what's going on.'

It was tough climbing. The escarpment consisted of loose shale and not much scrub to hold it together. He scrambled, sliding backwards sometimes and clawing for finger-and footholds until at last he reached the top, chest heaving. He lay until he had his breath under control and then, taking off his hat and with his army binoculars in his hand, he inched forward until he could see the trail ahead.

He swept the scene with his glasses.

The trail led into a valley. The stream that Charlie would get her water from widened as other tributaries streamed into it. The valley floor was flat and tall grasses grew up to where the forest began rearing up the valley sides.

Far away he could see puffs of smoke rising high in the air and he knew Ned Bascombe was caught between two angles of fire.

The wagon train was already encircled, with a milling mass of horses and cattle inside the ring. So Ned had been transporting several wealthy families by the look of things. Settlers they would be.

He ranged around and saw that the marauders were not Indians but white men. Rustlers, by God!

He watched for a few minutes and then scrambled down to Charlie. She looked at him.

'Well?'

'Not Indians. My guess is either rustlers or Comancheros. If it's Comancheros, they're well out of their

174

country. We'll know when we get there. Comancheros leave everyone dead and take the cash and everything they can carry away. Rustlers only want cattle and horses.'

Charlie looked frightened. 'You're not seriously going to go on? We could be killed!'

'Look, I've survived more skirmishes with the military than you've seen full moons. We'll not ride in openly. We'll belly our way in. Ned Bascombe can do with all the help he can get! Come on, Charlie, where's your guts? You stood up to those raiders when your pa died. Now you can follow me. I'll look after you.'

She looked at him with the big eyes of a frightened rabbit. 'What if they catch me, Buff?'

'I won't let them. I'd kill you first!'

She gulped. 'Couldn't we just turn round and ride away?'

'And hate ourselves afterwards? There's women and children down there. Do you want them on your conscience knowing we might have helped them?'

'But we're only two and I'm next to useless.'

'You can fire a gun and load, and help keep the womenfolk calm. That's helping.'

She bit her lip. 'I'm not brave, Buff, but I guess I'll just have to stick with you. I see I'm not going to change your mind.'

'You've no choice, kid. I'm going in, and if you don't, you could be in big trouble.' He put an arm about her. 'Believe me, love, it's for the best.'

Her head came up sharply. 'You called me love!'

'Yes . . . well . . . I think of you as love.'

'You do?' Her eyes gleamed, fright gone from them. The beginnings of a smile touched her lips. She took a deep breath. 'I don't think I'm frightened any more. What are we waiting for? Let's ride!'

They rode cautiously and when

they were within rifle range, they dismounted, tethered their horses under a thick stand of trees and made for a cluster of boulders.

McCall climbed swiftly to the top of the heap and took a look nothing the intense activity down below. So the defence was still strong.

The smell of cooped-up animals rose in the air, mingling with the stench of firearms. The sound of gunfire was dulled by the lowing of maddened cows and the screams of frightened horses. Two wagons were on fire, the grey smoke and orange flames crackling and spreading.

McCall swung his glasses around the circle of wagons. Already he could see bodies lying where they'd fallen. A young boy dangled over a wagon shaft.

He saw the flashes of gunfire from inside and under the remaining wagons and then his attention was drawn to the marauders. It was as he had thought. They were rustlers, out to take the cattle and horses. Already there had been a breach in the circle, and inside someone was directing most of the firing in defending that breach.

He also saw a place not defended and he knew that if he and Charlie could reach it, they could join the defenders.

The place was a niche in the hillside. A sheer wall rose above one of the wagons. It looked like a freight wagon and was not a target for the rustlers.

He made a decision. They could take a roundabout route and come down the hillside, belly down, and dive under the wagon. From then on it would be a matter of opportunity.

Down below, he explained to Charlie what must be done. She nodded, too strung-up to speak.

'We'll take every scrap of ammo with us, but before we do so, I'll make up a few surprise packets like the army do when they're up against it.' As he was speaking he was emptying cartridges into his kerchief and with quick sure hands adding a strip torn from his shirt, to make a fire bomb. He made several bundles.

'Give me a strip from your shirt, Charlie. This is the last one.' Silently she tugged and tore a strip from her shirt and handed it to him.

'Will it work, Buff?'

'When the strips are lighted, there'll be a big bang. Some work, some don't. The troops use them as a last resort. At least it gives the advantage of surprise. Now, we're ready. There'll be no talking and you're to do exactly as I do. I'll wave you on or stop you with a hand signal. You'll watch carefully and stick to me like shit to a blanket, do you hear?'

She nodded, once more trembling with fright of the unknown.

Then they moved forward carefully and when he dropped to his knees and crawled forward, she did the same. The shotgun she carried was heavy. It threatened to drag her down but she gritted her teeth and forced herself to keep up his pace.

The firing and yelling burgeoned into a maelstrom of sound and she knew then that they were nearly at their objective. A hand on her shoulder stopped her from bumping into McCall. She lay flat and breathed deeply to ease her lungs and aching muscles. She was nearly spent but she knew she must recover enough strength to make the last dash down the steep side of the valley and crawl under the freight wagon.

McCall tapped her twice on the shoulder and waved her forward. Now was the time to use every ounce of muscle, scramble through the grass and dive under the wagon.

Her spine tingled, expecting the impact of a bullet at any time and she was surprised when finally she rolled gasping under cover of the sheltering wagon.

McCall turned and looked at her. He grinned and she saw that he didn't see her as Charlie, the girl, but as Charlie, the boy. There was an aura about him, a wildness, a fighting spirit that was reckless. She could see that at this moment he feared nothing, not even dying.

She wished she could feel the same. Instead, she wet her pants.

She lay, the hot feeling between her legs gradually subsiding to a cold uncomfortable sogginess. For a moment it took her mind off their predicament. She was miserable, shivering with reaction, and exhausted.

He turned to her. He had to put his mouth to her ear to make her hear.

'Lie still. Don't come out until I come for you. I'm going to find Ned Bascombe. I'll be back.'

'But . . . '

He didn't hear her and was gone. The last she saw of him were his legs scrambling between the shafts of the wagon and disappearing under the next one.

She lay back and tried to pray but couldn't. She couldn't think of the right words to say. So she thought of

McCall and tried to put a protective shield about him, which was silly really, but the only thing she could think of to do.

The noise and screaming went on. Then she heard the pounding thunder of feet and knew the cows and horses had breached the gap and were now pouring out and stampeding down the valley.

The wagon train would be helpless without horses.

Then she heard explosions far down the valley. They came in quick succession, so she knew McCall must have contacted Ned. He couldn't have fired all those bundles himself.

She couldn't cower under the wagon for ever. She must get out and see what was happening. Close by all was quiet. She figured that the rustlers must now have turned their attention to the stampeding cattle.

She crawled from under the wagon and stood up. The scene was one of desolation. The central ground was churned up by the animals' feet. All around were wagons, some wrecked, some still intact, while two still burned fiercely. Already groups of men were dragging them by the shafts well away from the circle, to burn themselves out downwind from the rest. She saw women carrying small children into any shelter they could find. Some were bloodied, all worked silently at what they had to do.

A man salvaging goods from a wrecked wagon stopped and looked at her.

'You'll be the woman the halfbreed mentioned. He was sweaty and grimy and smelled of burnt gunpowder.

She nodded. 'What's happening now? Have the rustlers gone?'

'Yeh, they did what they'd come to do, drove off the cattle and horses. Ned and the halfbreed and some of the fellers not wounded have gone after them. The halfbreed had some kind of plan to turn the stampede around.' He wiped his bloody face and spat. 'We're lucky to have our lives. If it had been the Sioux, we would all be dead!'

'The explosions! You heard them? McCall's using them to turn the cows!'

'Is that his name, McCall?'

'Yes. He was an army scout and knows about gunpowder and how to make fire-bombs. The leading cows will turn and maybe . . . ' She stopped at the thought it conjured up. 'If it's done right, then they could engulf the rustlers who're driving them on!'

Charlie and the man stared at each other.

'By God, I reckon you've got the right of it!' He slapped his thigh and his shoulders straightened. 'Come and talk to the rest of the men. Maybe we should get the wagons ready to roll again. Maybe we'll get our horses back!'

Charlie explained to the crowd of men and women who listened to what she had to say. Then they went about their business with new heart. There were eight bodies to bury and goods not destroyed to be taken from wrecked wagons and stowed on other wagons and so all became overladen. But they were ready to roll if and when their men returned with the horses and such cattle as could be rounded up.

It was nightfall when the men returned, driving a herd of horses and a few cattle.

Ned Bascombe shook McCall by the hand. 'If it hadn't been for you, lad, we'd not even have one horse between us. As it is, we've lost a lot of horses and cows and what's worse, we've lost good men and women. But we'll carry on. We aim to reach California and by God we will! Are you coming with us?'

McCall shook his head. 'I'm not but she is. I want you to take her with you and find her good folks to live with.'

'McCall!'

He ignored her protest. 'Ned, you hear me? Find her a good home and here's my savings. A quarter for you and the rest for her. I trust you, feller.

Someday I'm going to check up and if you fail me . . . ' He paused and then said softly, 'I'll come after you and tear your balls off and make you eat them! Right?'

Ned Bascombe took the purse. It weighed heavy. He was too stunned to speak. He nodded. By God, he'd look after that girl as if she was his own! He wanted to die intact.

Then McCall was being engulfed by Charlie. She wound herself about him, clinging like a limpet.

'I want to go back with you, Buff! I won't be left behind!'

He kissed her on the mouth, feeling the warm trembling of her and then he tore her free and shoved her into Ned Bascombe's arms.

'Look to her, Ned. Tie her down if you have to, but take her to California!' Then he turned and walked away up the valley to find his tethered horse without looking at her again.

She screamed after him. 'I'll find you, Buff, wherever you go!'

He didn't look around. She collapsed on the ground crying noisily. Ned looked at her helplessly.

'I'll go fetch one of the women. She'll be a comfort to you.'

8

McCall rode hard for two days. He'd spent several hours by a stream, having bathed, refreshing himself and revelling in the cold water streaming from the faraway mountains.

He lived off the land, a jack-rabbit, a prairie turkey and, great luxury, a clutch of quail's eggs found in long grass.

He felt as one with the great silence. He breathed in, sniffing the pine-laden air like a prisoner just freed from jail. He could sense his oneness with the wild places. These untouched woodlands, this natural landscape were his true home. He wished he could just go where he willed, without a duty to the Sioux to hold him back.

He missed Charlie too.

Oh, how he missed her! His whole body ached for her. He couldn't believe how she'd entwined herself about his heart. He'd been a fool to let her go. Yet he stiffened his resolve. He justified himself. She was a white girl and as such must live among her own kind of people. She would never have survived the existence that he craved. She would never have understood the silences and moods of the great outback with only himself to cling to.

He grieved for her inwardly as if she was already dead, as she would be for ever to him.

His jaw hardened. His sacrifice of her was not to be in vain. He would seek out Broken Nose who should now be surrounding the Black Hills and fending off the invading hordes of adventurers who were streaming into the hills to find and dig holes for the gold that was hidden deep underground.

Already he'd seen the signs of movement and the dust clouds raised by wagons. The miners and adventurers were like locusts, too numerous and too determined, lusting with gold fever for the yellow metal and dreams of riches beyond imagination.

The thought of gold did not stir him. What stirred him was the thought that the ancient places, the many deep caverns with their faded pictures depicting sun worship, and their secret writings, were being violated.

One special place reminded him of his mother and her people and the beauty and holiness of the place she had taken him to receive a blessing from the gods.

He owed it to her to offer his right hand and his life in its defence.

He was surprised to come upon Broken Nose and his band of warriors which had doubled in number. As he approached the camp he saw that there were members of many more tribes mingling with the Sioux. The situation in Washington must have deteriorated.

Broken Nose greeted him with a raising of the hand.

'Ah, Warbuck! Greetings! We thought

you had forsaken us. Fox Catcher says you betrayed us to the White Eyes. Is this true?'

McCall glared in anger. 'Fox Catcher speaks with snake's tongue! I would never turn my back on you and what you stand for!'

'Why did you leave us?'

'To take my woman to safety. A warrior fights better when he has no woman worries. You should know that.'

Broken Nose nodded. 'I understand. The womenfolk are the backbone of the tribe. If they die, the tribe dies. Huh!'

'I see you have doubled your men. Has Red Cloud sent word for the final onslaught?'

Broken Nose shook his head. 'We still wait, but harass the newcomers. Some have turned back whence they came which is good. We think the old man is getting soft, and bows to the wishes of the White Eyes too much! If word does not come soon, we shall attack every military fort in the Dakotas!'

'It would mean many deaths!'

'Better to fight and die with honour than to become some crawling insect!'

'Perhaps you are right. How long will you wait?'

'We wait until the next new moon and if we do not get a message from Red Cloud, we'll make our own plan of attack!'

But Broken Nose's battle plan never came to fruition. On the third day, a lookout came bounding down the rocks waving his arms and crying, 'Aryeeh! Aryee-ee-eh! The white chief comes with his troops!'

McCall, hearing the cry, scaled the escarpment and lay belly down as he scanned the vista before him.

He saw a huge dust cloud snaking away into the distance. He also saw wisps of smoke as other Sioux bands sent up their warning signals. He adjusted his binoculars and saw the long columns of riders, their equipment and the wagons carrying not one but three of the new fire-belching Gatling guns. It was going to be the mother and father of battles. The fate of the Black Hills was going to be decided in the next few days!

He scrambled down and reported to Broken Nose, emphasizing the presence of the big guns.

'You've got your answer, Chief. Those guns spell out the message from Washington. Gold comes before legal settlements.'

Chief Broken Nose nodded slowly. 'So be it! It is war!'

There was a commotion amongst the watching crowd of braves. They parted and watched as two young braves struggled with a prisoner, dragging him, kicking wildly, and threw him down at the feet of McCall and the chief.

'We found the boy skulking in the forest. We brought him in because he cannot be a spy.'

Another brave led a horse by its bridle. McCall gasped as he recognized the horse and the prisoner, who lay with bound wrists and a gag across the face.

'Charlie?'

Broken Nose looked at him with a peculiar quirk to his lips as if he would have laughed in better times. 'It seems as if my men have captured your woman!'

McCall lunged forward and dragged Charlie to her feet. 'What in hell are you doing here?' He ripped off her gag and cut her hands free.

'I told you I should find you!' She flung up her head and looked at him defiantly. 'I didn't watch you tracking for nothing! It was easy. You didn't try to hide your trail!'

'By God, I should whip you, you madheaded stupid bitch! I could kill you!' Then he grabbed her in his arms and held her close.

Broken Nose turned away, and at a gesture from him so did all his men.

McCall rocked Charlie to him. 'Oh! God, Charlie, you're the very devil but I've missed you! God, how I've missed you!'

'So you won't kill me?' Her voice held a hint of laughter.

He sighed. 'You're the most head-strong woman I've ever known! All I wanted was for you to be safe and happy.'

'I'll be safe and happy with you.'

He shook her, but carefully as if she was something precious and fragile.

'Do you know what you've let yourself in for?'

'I don't care. Where you go, I go. Home will be where you are. Don't you realize that?'

He stared down at her. 'I think you really mean that.'

'I've said it often enough. Now do you believe me?'

His answer was to hug her close and kiss her forehead. 'We'll make a new life as soon as this is over. We'll not stay with the Sioux. We'll strike out into the wilds and find a new home away from strife and civilization. That's what I want, and that is what will happen. Do you want that, Charlie? Could you live your life with me alone?'

She looked up at him, trusting. 'I've followed you for days on my own, fended for myself. If I can do that, I can live quite happily with you. Trust me, Buff.'

'Right. We'll see this out together, and if the spirits will it, I'll take you to my mother's sacred place and we'll unite in love and pledge our troth and then we shall go and seek our new home!'

★ ★ ★

The clash came two days later. The hills and the lonely places were filled with the sounds of artillery fire and rifle shooting and behind it all the distant call of a bugle.

The Sioux were ready and waiting. In front of them were the oncoming troops. Behind them, they defended

196

the foothills leading up to the sacred Black Hills, looking sombre now with their coating of lofty pines that gave the hills their name.

From all the outcroppings of rock, McCall knew that the Sioux, the Cheyenne and the lesser tribes were waiting. All the bands had their orders. Stand firm or die.

McCall had hastily taken Charlie to his mother's sacred place. It was not how he'd envisaged it, this hasty visit and leave-taking. But he stood in the spot where he and his mother had stood all those years ago, and he'd prayed for her and for Charlie and himself.

Then he'd clasped her close and kissed her. 'I love only you, Charlie. If I live when this battle is over, I'll come for you, for you're the one I want to spend the rest of my life with.'

'And if you don't come back?'

'Pray for me and the Sioux will see you get back amongst your own people.'

He turned and left her and he heard her calling as he rode away.

The battle was savage. The Gatling guns mounted on three hills spat out bullets from all angles. The losses were great and yet the united tribes refused to move back. Their marksmen hidden amongst the rocks aimed and fired automatically and the men grunted with satisfaction when they saw a trooper throw up his arms and fall to the ground.

Two suicide squads moved in to silence the thunderfire guns and succeeded. The third was on a high plateau and couldn't be reached.

Through the smoke McCall could see the last Gatling gun fanning out, spitting death as it went, yet wave after wave of mounted warriors rode bareback, clinging to their horses' ribs and on a side away from the enemy, spitting out their own death to the unwary.

McCall watched the trail of death. The last big gun must be silenced. He started to climb the escarpment at the back of the gun. The battle cry went up as he did so to cheer him on.

'Aryeeeh! Aryeeeah! Warbuck! Warbuck!' The officer in charge of the flanking movement against the hostiles, heard the cry.

'What devil's business are those goddamned bastards up to?' Colonel Carrington growled to his captain of artillery.

'I don't know, Colonel, but whatever it means, it's put new heart into the demons from hell! Should I order a withdrawal, sir? To regroup, sir? We've lost a lot of men and we're covering our ground too thinly.'

'Like hell we will! We don't retreat. We stand our ground and fight, Captain! That's what we're here for!'

'But, sir . . . '

'You heard me, soldier! Get the bugler and sound the advance! We take 'em and break 'em, Captain, or die trying!'

'Yessir!'

The captain turned away to summon the bugler and suddenly a spurt of blood stained his uniform jacket. He gasped and then crumpled. Colonel Carrington cursed. He'd lost a good artillery officer.

McCall mounted the crag above the Gatling gun's position. Two shots and the soldier cranking the gun's mechanism blasted off the plateau, plummeting to the ground below. Another shot and one of the service crew fell to the ground. McCall fired again at a burly man who looked like a sergeant, the last of the crew, but this time the trigger clicked on an empty barrel.

He flung it aside and leapt at the man facing him down below. His weight knocked the soldier to the ground and then they were grappling each other, rolling over and over, snarling and biting and gouging.

The soldier had a knife in his hand. McCall grabbed his wrist and they fought chest to chest, first one and then the other straining to sink the knife into his adversary.

McCall felt the blade at his throat, pricking and drawing blood; then, heaving and stretching, he pushed it aside. The knife trembled between them as each strained to give the final blow.

McCall's strength was failing. The big man's bull strength was fast overcoming him. Then as he kicked out, he brought up his knee and caught the soldier in the crotch.

The man screamed and cursed and tried to roll away. McCall, quick as a flash, straddled him and turned the man's wrist. His weight drove the knife into the soldier's heart.

The man's eyes widened and blood poured from his mouth. McCall sprang away from him and staggered to the machine gun.

For a long moment the world spun around. When it settled he found himself cranking the handle of the lethal gun, which had six barrels and spat out its message of death.

Like a maniac, McCall whipped the gun round so that it pointed in the direction of the troops. Then he fanned it as he cranked like a drunken man. He closed his eyes at the unfolding carnage.

For a moment he remembered his father and was ashamed; then he brushed away the thought. He was doing this for his mother and for what she believed in.

At last the belt of bullets was emptied and he sank down on the ground, sickened with what he'd done. Those men had had no chance. But then, neither had the Indians. But he still felt ashamed.

He looked down at the scene of the bloodiest battle he'd ever been in and that was when he saw her.

He leaned over the ledge and watched with horror. Charlie was being dragged by two troopers towards a man he recognized.

Colonel Henry Carrington!

What in God's name was he doing here with his troop?

Then he had it. Washington had ordered a complete massacre of all the tribes involved in the dispute.

He stood upright and yelled the Sioux war cry. He waved his hands, then, in a piercing cry, yelled to Colonel Carrington.

'Colonel! You want me! Let the girl go and I'll come down to you. If not, I'll fire this gun again!' He looked down and saw the piled-up belts of bullets. It would be easy to load up and fire.

He also saw movement out of sight of those down below. Broken Nose, bloody but still strong on his feet, and Fox Catcher were climbing up to him.

'I'm warning you, Colonel. Let the girl go!'

'You wouldn't dare!' yelled back the colonel. 'Would you kill her too?'

'She would understand.'

He saw her struggle and try to bite

the trooper's wrist. She turned and spat something at the colonel.

'She says you must give yourself up. She doesn't want to die!'

'He's a lying bastard, Buff. I've just told him to go to hell!' Charlie yelled. 'Do it, Buff! I love you. I always will!'

McCall motioned to Fox Catcher. 'Feed the belt in there. Quickly now!'

Fox Catcher stared at him. 'You would kill your woman?'

'You heard her. Quickly now.'

The two Indians moved clumsily but managed to load the fearsome weapon.

McCall took aim over the heads of the troops and gave an experimental crank to check that they had loaded properly. It gave a hiccup and a splat and a stream of bullets arced into the air.

He looked over the edge at the colonel. 'You believe me now, Colonel? The next time I fire it will be at you and everyone around you.'

'You no-good halfbreed bastard! I always said you were an animal! Worse than an animal. An animal who can think! I'll let her go if you will come down here and face me like a man, or are you too cowardly to do that?'

McCall laughed. 'Let me see her go first. Charlie, run to your left and you'll be with friends. Well, Colonel, do you free her?'

The colonel did not answer but nodded to the troopers. They let her go. She turned and spat in the colonel's face and ran for cover.

The colonel wiped his face. 'Bitch!' but she'd disappeared into the scrub. McCall relaxed. Then the colonel looked up at McCall. 'Well? Are you satisfied?'

For answer, McCall shoved the machine gun belt into Fox Catcher's hands and nodded to Broken Nose to take over the crank handle. In turn, the Indians offered him their knives with a silent nod of encouragement.

McCall smiled grimly. He would

need all the good luck he could get, for he was conscious of aching muscles and the slow pounding in his head.

Then he was slithering and sliding down to the ground below. He walked with firm lithe footsteps to within a dozen feet of the colonel.

'I'm here. What are you going to do about it?'

The colonel gave a yell and lunged forward, swinging his sabre and using it like a cutting knife.

'I'll get you, you bastard,' he ground out between clenched teeth. 'I should have had you killed years ago, traitor!'

Anger boiled in McCall but he kept strict control of his temper. Losing control meant mistakes but if the colonel wanted to rave, let him. It only needed one mistake on Carrington's part.

He sprang to the side as the colonel's lunge sent him off balance, and narrowly missed tearing the officer's shoulder. They both swung round, panting and lunging, McCall now in a crouch, both knives glinting in the dying sun.

He balanced on the balls of his feet, a moving target for the thrusts and charges of the flashing sabre, the man's face a twisted grimace which reminded McCall of a wounded wolf.

He watched the eyes, hate-filled and flickering, and, as the wild lunges came faster and faster, got their full measure. He was a lot younger than the colonel but he was tiring after his earlier battle and knew that the end would come soon.

He caught the colonel in the biceps and then again on the shoulder blade, but each time he was too late to drive the knife deeply.

Sweat was now pouring from the colonel and his own blood was seeping down his arm making his sword arm sticky and slippery. 'Goddamn you, McCall!' he shouted. 'Too afraid of my blade to stand and fight?' He followed up with a swing of the sabre and then a counter swing which nearly took McCall by surprise. He drew blood. Another inch and he would have pierced McCall's heart.

'Very well, if you want it that way.' McCall laughed and crouched ready, waiting . . . When it came, the slashing blade was whipped from the colonel's hand. It clattered to the ground behind him.

For a moment the colonel stood stunned. He passed a shaking hand over his eyes.

'So, what will you do now? Murder me and become a wanted killer?'

McCall drew several gasping breaths. 'I could do that and no one would ever know, but I'm not a wild beast, Colonel. You can keep your miserable life!' He turned his back, cleaning his knives on his sleeve.

It was then that the colonel made a dive for a revolver lying by a dead soldier. He lay on the ground, twisting rapidly and firing at McCall's back. McCall heard the click of the trigger and the shot hit him in the shoulder.

The blast flung him to the ground.

The colonel scrambled upright and, gun swinging in his hand, came to stand over him, laughing. He turned him over with his toe and looked down at him.

'I told you I would get you, McCall, so take a last good look around, halfbreed before you meet your Maker!'

McCall stared up at him, pain in his arm drowning the feeling of fear. He could only think of Charlie and what might have been. At least she was safe . . .

Then the blast came. Both men had forgotten the Indians up above with the Gatling gun. Now it spelled out death as the stream of bullets cut the colonel in half.

It was a good day to die for some.

★ ★ ★

McCall opened his eyes and saw Charlie's face above him. He felt weak

209

and he was bandaged up tightly. He was also in a tepee that was redolent of herbs and garlic and decoctions that smelled ghastly. He was parched and wanted a drink.

'How long have I been on my back?' he croaked, his tongue trying to wet dry lips.

Charlie lifted his head and he tasted cool water. He drank.

'Long enough to be out of all the negotiations that have been going on. The battle's over, Buff. Red Cloud persuaded the men in Washington to renew the contract and the Black Hills are ceded again to the Indians. The tribes are making arrangements to go on the reservations, Buff. Isn't that good news?'

He stared up at her.

'You think so?'

'Yes. There will be peace and that must be good.'

McCall shook his head wearily.

'You think the sacred hills won't be mined? Once the white men get a taste of gold, they'll be back! You'll see.'

'But that will not worry us, Buff. We'll do as you want. Go right away to a new land and find our own place where it is peaceful and happy.'

He struggled to sit up. She put a pillow to his back and he held her close.

'You still want that?'

'Of course. What you want, I want.'

He hugged her close. 'The first thing we do when I get on my feet is go to my mother's sacred place. We shall promise ourselves to each other for ever and ever, and we shall cleave unto each other until death do us part.'

'Yes, we'll do that, Buff McCall, and then we'll go into the unspoiled wilderness and find the special place waiting for us and make it our own!'

He looked up at her and laughed. How could he have ever even contemplated parting with her?

It was a question he could never answer.

Epilogue

After Red Cloud's Peace Settlement it would take eight years before the Indian troubles finally came to a head. In the meantime the Sioux and the Cheyenne had many skirmishes with adventurers and gold seekers who came and cleared land, chopping down trees for the timber needed for pit-props and mines.

There were many deaths on both sides, and much misery for the Indians, for their hunting grounds were being demolished and their way of life torn apart.

The great clash came in 1876 when surveyors found rich deposits of gold in the Black Hills and once more the government reneged on the deal with the Indians.

The treaty stipulating that all of the country of the North Platte, through the Black Hills to the summit of the Big

Horn Mountains was to be considered Indian territory, was broken.

Then came the battle on the banks of the Little Big Horn River, which became known as 'Custer's Last Stand' and also 'The Last Stand of the Sioux Indians'.

The Indians won that great battle but in doing so they lost the war.

Sitting Bull and Crazy Horse, who had taken command, were never allowed to celebrate that victory, for the troops under command of General Miles harassed and pursued them so much that the Indians had no time to hunt for food for their families.

General Miles's tactics paid off. In time, Sitting Bull and Crazy Horse had to negotiate a surrender or starve to death.

Reluctantly, the tribes moved into the reservations and became reliant on the food rations doled out by the Indian agencies.

The proud Indians, natives of the country, were brought to their knees.

The White Eyes, the strangers, would now shape their future.

Other titles in the
Linford Western Library:

THE BOUNTYMEN

Tom Anson

Tom Quinlan headed a bunch of other bounty hunters to bring in the long-sought Dave Cull, who was not expected to be alone. That they would face difficulties was clear, but an added complication was the attitude of Quinlan's strong-minded woman, Belle. And suddenly, mixed up in the search for Cull, was the dangerous Arn Lazarus and his men. Hunters and hunted were soon embroiled in a deadly game whose outcome none could predict.

THE EARLY LYNCHING

Mark Bannerman

Young Rice Sheridan leaves behind his adoptive Comanche parents and finds work on the Double Star Ranch. Three years later, he and his boss, Seth Early, are ambushed by outlaws, and their leader, the formidable Vince Corby, brutally murders Early. Rice survives and reaches town. Pitched into a maelstrom of deception and treachery, Rice is nevertheless determined that nothing will prevent him from taking revenge on Corby. But he faces death at every turn . . .